SAVE THE BONSAI

Save the Bonsai

By
Aaron Aalborg

ISBN: 9781794365018

Cover design by Sabertooth Books

Acknowledgements

Thanks are due to Bob Brashears for excellent editing, Calvin Cahail for cover design and beta readers: Kevin Francis Ryan, Galya Gerstman, John Wayne Blount, Kate Stanger and Martin Zucker. Additional advice was given by the members of two supportive writers' groups here in Costa Rica and from my ever-patient wife, Ivy, who finds my plots too violent, but helps anyway.

All profits from this book will go to charity.

All the author's previous profits went to the charity Oxfam. Following the scandals surrounding that organization and failure of all its leaders to accept responsibility and resign, payments there were suspended. They may resume on the departure of the chairman. Until then, profits will go to non-denominational charities with low administration costs, effective in getting aid to the needy in the developing world.

Foreword

This fantasy, sci-fi thriller opens with a person of uncertain gender. The suffering of such people is a consequence of an accident of birth. My character, Daremo, is based on a true story, related to me by a social worker friend. The location and names are disguised to protect those involved. The subsequent life of Daremo herein is fiction.

Researching what personal pronoun to use for a no-gender person proved unsatisfactory. "They" is preferred by some but implies a plural. When one moves on to other forms of pronoun, e.g. possessives, things get ever more complicated

Some activists, most of whom are not transgender, think they have the right to dictate what becomes standard usage. After looking at many options, I consulted the social worker, who had told me the true story of the person I used as the basis for the character, Daremo in this novel. The base character for Daremo preferred "s/he." It therefore seemed right to use that. If this is overwhelmingly upsetting to anyone, tough! No one dictates English usage. It emerges through a Darwinian selection. There are more important world issues to worry about.

Characters/Dramatis Personae

The Humans

Professor Daremo - Daremo is not a usual Japanese name. It means “no one”. Daremo plays a dark role in this tale. “S/he” was born without visible sexual organs. The resulting suffering drives an inexorable anger, fury and a thirst for vengeance. Daremo’s birth parents, adoptive parents and twin appear briefly in our story. Is s/he an arch villain or a victim with understandable reactions?

Aiko Okamoto - Daremo’s twin.

Drs. Okamoto - A husband and wife, who adopt Aiko and Daremo.

Carrie Gomez - Anchor interviewer for the online, underground publication *Hacking Today*.

Bruce Kárpov - Bruce is a hacker. He becomes Number One on the FBI's most wanted list. He is the infamous founder of the Save the Bonsai movement.

Sunshine, aka Judy Bluestein - Bruce's friend and more.

Dave Gonosz - A former green beret, a very violent man and organizer of others.

Liza Angelou - An FBI Special Agent.

General Chuck Carver – A retired Ranger, who founded and owns a multi-national security company.

Japanese Sex Workers

Sekushina Josei– Meaning Sexy Woman.

Babi Ningyo - Meaning Barbie Doll.

More will emerge concerning these last two.

<<>>

There are Minor Roles - Social workers, keepers of archives, housekeepers, and others.

The Plants

In many ways, plants are the stars of this tale. My imagination was electrified by the BBC documentary "How Plants Communicate and Think." British national treasure, naturalist and wild life documentary maker, David Attenborough's "Plants Behaving Badly," about carnivorous species, cemented my fascination. There is much serious scientific research available on plant sentience. They, make sounds, sense in totally different ways than humans, respond, communicate, and remember. We cannot even understand what dolphins are saying, so it is no surprise that science on organisms without animal brains and neurological systems is at a primitive, but fascinating stage.

Rattan - Is the common term for a jungle creeper endemic to Southeast Asia. Anyone who has been caught by its backward pointing spines whilst walking jungle trails will attest to the pain. It hooks into clothing and flesh. It is best avoided. If caught, careful backward steps must be taken for release. Forward movement drives the spines farther in. Indigenous people use the stems as a source of water. They cut a length and drink from the bottom. They also eat its fruit. After the spines are removed, they weave it into intricate and durable furniture, basketry, and fish traps.

Poisonous species - There are thousands of plants and fungi containing varying amounts of toxins. These can be distributed by direct contact, ingestion, in water or as airborne particles or gasses. Only some plant characters are named. Antiaris toxicaria is a large tree, common in the tropics. Its sap, mixed with other plant substances, makes a lethal tip for poisoned darts, fired from blowpipes and arrows used by indigenous peoples.

Grasses - Bamboo is the tallest and fastest growing grass in the world. It offers amazing strength and flexibility. It has been widely used as scaffolding, flooring material, in construction, and for art in Asia. More recently its use in clothing, biodegradable eating utensils and dishware are becoming popular.

Carnivores - These species need nutrients unavailable to them from the poor soils in the locations they grow.

Sundew - Sticky sweet globules lure insects to its leaves. They become stuck. The leaf curls around them and they are digested.

Venus flytrap - These are often grown as interesting, tiny houseplants. Insects are attracted to the open leaves by color and taste. Touching two of the little hairs within the open leaf triggers the plant to close in a fraction of a second, trapping prey for ingestion.

Pitcher plants - Often spectacularly beautiful, they are native to areas of the U.S. and Asia and come in many varieties. Some are quite large. Their leaves form a vase-like structure, holding a digestive liquid in the base. The inner part of their overhanging tops is attractive to their prey in color and taste. The insect, frog or small mammal starts to feed on the plant's tasty excrescences. Then it cannot climb out, due to a waxy inner surface and downward pointing hairs. Prey falls into the digestive juices.

Mobile species - Most plants are highly mobile. They cover most of the planet, so this must be true. Their movements are usually slow, if measured in human timescale. Movement can be seen through time lapse photography. Most grow upwards seeking light or other plants to climb upon. Their roots grow toward water and nutrients. Some spread through underground rhizomes. Others use aerial roots. Yet more are blown along by the wind. Tumbleweed and winged seed pods can move very rapidly.

Many species attract, insects, animals, and birds to feed on their pollens and fruits to spread them far and wide.

Bonsai - Although the word most in use today is Japanese, the Chinese were the first to develop the art of growing miniature trees in restrictive containers, “pun- sai”, around 700 AD.

CHAPTER 1

In an unexplored canyon

On the slopes of Mount Kinabalu,

The tropical Island of Borneo

Borneo is the largest island in Asia. It lies across the Equator, close to Indonesia, which most of it is a part. The rest is ruled by Malaysia and Brunei. Much of Borneo is still unexplored, a land of impenetrable steaming jungles, high mountains, and headhunting tribes with animist religions. Recently the oldest cave paintings in the world were discovered there.

Borneo's highest mountain is Kinabalu, at over 4,000 meters, or 13,000 feet elevation. It is fringed with vertiginous canyons. Many are so remote, deep, and difficult to access that they are not yet fully explored.

In the shadows, squats Daremo, a lone, androgynous figure, hunched over a powerful spotting scope. An expensive, auto-stabilized camera is mounted on a nearby tripod in the shadowy mouth of a small cave. The dark cavern-mouth is halfway up a deep gorge. It provides a discrete viewing point for the steep wall of dense vegetation and rocky outcrops a bowshot across the gorge.

It is impossible to determine whether the photographic equipment is operated by a man or a woman. S/he stares intently at a specific object, halfway up the thick tropical jungle across the canyon. The noon sun is finally chasing away the clammy mists and sticky shadows, as it peeps over the rim of the ravine, far above. The human figure relaxes a little. *This light is perfect for photography, as long as the humidity does not cloud my lenses.*

Daremo's dark Japanese eye is glued to the optic. S/he licks thin lips in anticipation. Breathing is sniper slow now. A sensitive finger hovers over the remote button to start filming. There is a fleeting smile of triumph.

Enduring days of trekking through the tropical undergrowth finally proved worthwhile. Native guides hacked a difficult and hazardous trail. S/he used the journey to observe and record interesting plant species. That almost made up for the hardships. The flesh tearing spines of rattan creepers dug deeper in when s/he tried to walk on when snagged. S/he found that the only way out was to step back and extract the vicious barbs very carefully.

Nonetheless, they left painful and itching wounds in the flesh. They festered unless treated.

In a sheltered stream, Daremo bathes, away from the prying eyes of the local guides. S/he is ashamed of a genderless body. A huge swarm of black bees descends on naked flesh, sucking up the salt sweat. S/he stays calm, so as not to provoke them. Ducking under the surface clears them off, but when dressing, s/he feels thousands of them crawling under pants and shirt. The guides from the nomadic Penan people laugh gleefully as s/he struggles frantically to get them out; scratching and swatting.

Scowling, s/he walks carefully away from the river, following the tribesmen's' silent, barefoot steps along the trail. Eventually, the swarm abandons its human salt lick to return to the hive.

Next day, s/he is riveted to the spot, observing a tribesman make slits in the bark of a substantial canopy tree to collect its latex-like sap in a bamboo vessel. S/he identifies the tree as Antiaris toxicaria. That evening in camp, Daremo watches, fascinated. The wizened Penan shaman with huge holes in his ear lobes to accommodate missing ornaments, ritually cooks the sap over low heat in a container fashioned from a leaf. A couple of hours later, he mixes the now thick and dark sap in a half-coconut bowl with other ingredients from his small leather pouch. S/he watches as he dips the sharp tips of several bamboo darts into the mixture.

Another tribesman fashions tiny wooden plugs to fletch the blunt ends. These fit exactly into the long blow pipes, allowing a puff of air to fire them accurately up to 15 meters. In Pidgin-English the Shaman tells Daremo, that even the tiniest prick from a poisoned dart means death. S/he realizes that his is a dying skill. The Penan are being driven from the diminishing Borneo jungle, by loggers and cultivation for palm oil.

The following morning, the chief blows a dart into a chattering monkey high above. When the missile first strikes its shoulder, the animal takes little notice. Irritated, it merely tugs it from the wound, tossing it aside. After some minutes, it gives a dry retch. Then, it tumbles from the tree, stone dead. The guides cook and eat the flesh without ill effects. Daremo enjoys a thigh.

S/he persuades the Penan headman to provide a dried sample of the poison for further analysis, thinking, *This hardy tree is common in the tropics. Its DNA may be useful to add to my plants' arsenal.*

When they finally arrive at the unexplored canyon, Daremo peers gingerly over the rim into the darkness. Butterflies flutter in Daremo's stomach at the thought of rappelling down to the cave's entrance. The guides explain that the opening is only a long rope-length below.

Once in the cave, Daremo suffers a week-long wait. Muscles are cramped and aching. Bats have sprayed their stinking urine and droppings before swarming out for their night hunt. S/he endures all this, interminable sweats, and hordes of biting insects. At last, the perfect moment arrives.

With tired eyes, from hours of intense staring through the spotter scope, s/he mutters. "No one else will ever see this film. It will become part of my highly personal and secret research project."

<<>>

With quiet satisfaction, Daremo reviews a vengeful plan. *The world will suffer the full, terrible results soon enough. This will be just payback for the humiliation and torments inflicted on me, an innocent person. My birth parents rejected me, simply because I was born without gender. They just dumped me. They've already paid for that.*

My early life was horrific. The parents who adopted me were inhuman monsters. When finally freed from them, merciless bullying and teasing were incessant, both in the classroom and at play. I've had my revenge on my despicable adoptive parents. Soon, it will be the turn of everyone else. No one will expect the nature of my gruesome retribution.

<<>>

On the opposite, vertiginous jungle-wall a squabbling troop of macaques is chattering as they feed near the spotting scope's crosshairs. An almost mature monkey strays into the view of the telescopic lens. Its red face turns toward Daremo. *It looks almost human, alert and inquisitive.* It bends to lick the sweet dew produced by the enormous pitcher plant. S/he gives it full attention. Exultant, s/he readies the remote-control button for the camera. *This is a new plant species for sure.*

<<>>

Daremo was fired in disgrace by the University of Tokyo for hacking into and stealing the research files of botanists and neuroscientists at Harvard and MIT. Before then, s/he was already hated and perhaps feared by colleagues as a freak of nature. Then s/he vanished for several years.

Two months before establishing the observation post in the cave, the professor left a hidden laboratory and private growing area in Tottori prefecture, Japan. It was disguised as an agricultural research station.

Tottori lies on the southern part of the north coast of Honshu, the largest Japanese Island. It has the sparsest population density in the country, ideal for clandestine activities.

It took Daremo ten grueling hours to reach Tokyo's Narita airport from there. Driving to the provincial capital's airport by back-roads, to avoid detection, was the hardest part.

<<>>

Daremo had undergone extensive plastic surgery. This allowed passage through the latest face recognition software at toll roads and airports. It enabled travel on false documents. It provided Daremo with the freedom to travel internationally, whilst breaking multiple laws prohibiting environmental damage and the transportation of rare species.

There were lengthy surgical procedures involved, adding a little flesh to the brows, bulking up the jaw-line and rounding-out the cheeks. Various wigs and protruding false teeth and skin dyes provided additional flexibility. The plastic surgeon mysteriously disappeared shortly after completing the treatments. Her records were destroyed in a fire. The media lamented another senseless fatality caused by a Japanese traditional wooden house. The fire service concluded that a votive candle ignited a Shinto shrine in the building. This had rapidly spread to the rest of the structure.

<<>>

Borneo's Nepenthes Rajah was previously considered the world's largest species of pitcher plant. It can contain as much as half a gallon of digestive fluid. That is easily enough to drown frogs, mice and large insects, before ingesting their nutrients. There were even reports of small rats. Daremo smiles. *This new plant on the opposite slope is similar in shape, but at least three times the size!*

Face flushed with the thrill s/he exultantly compares its field marks to the Rajah's. *There's the same red top, folded over like a cap to half cover the opening. This cap sweats sweet nectar-like beads. Its victims relish these as they are lured to their doom. The tall vase-like lower part of the plant is far larger than the Rajah's. It's almost half the size of an oil drum. As far as I can tell from here, the red slippery interior carries on downwards. Externally, this pitcher differs from the Rajah's blood- red color. The vase is banana yellow, with an intricate filigree lacework of pure white veins wrapped around it. These catch the light and really make the plant stand out. It's truly beautiful. I absolutely must possess it!*

<<>>

The macaque screams a desperate wail that echoes eerily across the canyon as it tumbles in head first. Fingers and toes scrabble hopelessly at the greasy interior. Panicking, it gasps into the enzyme rich juices that fill the base of the pitcher and drowns. Its dying cries are stifled. These liquids will break down its corpse into nutrients.

Enthralled, and without empathy for a fellow primate, Daremo stares in satisfaction until the huge flower ceases vibrating. Then s/he stops filming and packs up all of the gear. *It'll take me all day to descend, cross the bottom of the canyon and climb to that pitcher plant. It could take a few further days to observe and record the complete digestion of the animal. Then the plant has to be carefully collected, packed and smuggled back into Japan.*

Reflecting on the new species' spectacular beauty, Daremo daydreams. *I can modify your genes to make you much bigger and faster growing. Then, we'll see what you can trap. What shall I call you my pretty one? Maybe, "Nepenthes Terribilis."*

Wait till you meet my other plant friends my voracious, cutie. Plants never betray me. I can add so much to their lives. I only respect humans who work to help plants. All others are just there to be used and discarded.

CHAPTER 2

FBI Headquarters

The J. Edgar Hoover Building

935 Pennsylvania Avenue

Washington, D.C.

Special Agent Liza Angelou is studying the transcript of a webcast anchored by Carrie Gomez of "Hacking Today." Angelou is an attractive African American. Male team members, and some females, fantasize about her from a distance. Their discretion is wise. She is known to have kneed a colleague so hard in the groin when he made an inappropriate remark that he had to take a few days off.

She wrinkles her brow to focus on the document. *I need to understand what motivates this guy.*

Carrie: "Today, we're lucky enough to talk with the elusive Bruce
Kárpov, visionary, webmaster, and creator of 'Save the Bonsai.' He is number one on the FBI's most-wanted list. Bruce, let me start by asking you how you would describe Save the Bonsai?"

Bruce: "How about it being the worst mistake of my life, Carrie?"

Carrie (Chuckling): "Come on Bruce. It's made you world famous and the leader of a global phenomenon. Everyone wants to meet you, especially the feds, (laughs). Many want to be you."

Bruce: "Alright then, Save the Bonsai began as a protest movement, with a blog and website. It's morphed into a global activist group. Like many of these things in life, it grew way out of control.

"I want to make this absolutely clear. Protestors, and even terrorists, are doing all sorts of illegal stuff that has nothing to do with either Bonsai or me. They've done more harm than good. But that's all I'm saying about that—for my own safety."

Carrie: "You're talking about some elements of the hacking group, 'Anonymous,' and the self-styled Bonsai Liberation Army or BLA."

Bruce: "Like I said. I'm saying zip about those people, other than they have nothing to do with me."

Carrie: "Well let's just agree that 'these' people were inspired by your original ideas and blog."

<<>>

In a seedy motel in Elmsford, 20 miles north of New York City, Bruce was reviewing this earlier interview on a laptop. The motel was conveniently located in case he needed to make a fast getaway; just off the 287 Cross-Westchester Expressway. From there, speedy access to New York City, New Jersey and Connecticut was possible. The guest register for this dump showed his signature as Joe Garton.

He X'd out of the webcast on his laptop. Letting out a deep sigh, his head fell into his hands. *Maybe I should have told the truth? Then maybe not. The truth can be dangerous.*

Raising his head, he looked at his haggard reflection in the mirror behind the laptop. *Wow, I'm a mess. Looks as though I've not slept for days. Need a shave too.*

He found it cathartic to dwell on the interview he would have liked to have given Carrie Fischer. Reminiscing about his past was bittersweet. Why not indulge himself?

How would the interview I would have liked to give be? Maybe like this:

Carrie: "Bruce, what strange karma led to your worldwide notoriety?"

Me: "Well, I must say, I wish the thought'd never entered my head. In truth, I was bored and getting worried… It all started eight years ago. I was twenty-four and a hopeless nerd. I still am. My PhD program at Caltech was increasingly tedious. Seeking excitement and fortune, me and a few friends were hacking and playing hide and seek with the cyber police. They're everywhere, trying to control those on the dark web. Leading them a merry dance is a real buzz."

Carrie: "Something must have happened before that?"

Me: "I could give the excuse that my dad left us when I was fifteen. Actually, Mom kicked him out because he was drinking all the housekeeping money and couldn't hold down a job.

"After that, Mom had too many men friends coming around for my liking. I took bribes to go out, but that interfered with my time on the web. So, I moved out, sharing an apartment with other geeks. We paid our way through college by selling some of our hacking programs, dealing a little white powder, and writing term papers for rich kids.

Carrie: "What motivated you at that point?"

Me: "The thing that really got to me was—I wanted sex—not a girlfriend— just sex. This proved difficult. I must admit, I'm out of shape and ugly now. Okay, so I was never in shape. I was as attractive as a three-day-old pizza. Sports never made my agenda; too puny you see. Hacking and hoping to design a killer computer game became obsessions. That last never happened. The hacking went pretty well though, at least for a while."

Carrie: "What do you like about hacking?"

Me: "There's nothing like the high you get when you break into systems at the NSA, CIA or NASA. You can really mess with their heads, moving satellites and deleting or changing files. They're all military nuts. So, if you feed their paranoia, they can be panicked into completely closing down un-hacked systems. Defeating the overpaid, arrogant kids from Harvard and Princeton who work for Gates, Bezos and their like, is also deeply satisfying.

“Then there’s the fun and games, as they all rush around like headless chickens trying to find out who’s doing this. Course, you give ’em what they want to believe. Routing things through the Ukraine, Russia, North Korea or China usually does the trick and causes more mayhem.”

Carrie: “What changed?”

Me: “Okay, so now I am, twenty-eight. Even less chance of a girlfriend as my hair’s already starting to fall out. That’s one of life’s dirty tricks. As the zits go, so does the hair. Masturbation was the only sex I ever got. Still, better than nothing.

"One day, I'm at the grocery store and things come to a climax. It's the wrong sort unfortunately. My iPhone buzzes. The text reads. 'FBI in yr hse. Run!'

"Course, the first thing I did was ditch the phone. Everyone knows that Apple sold their users out years ago and can track you anywhere. I had just $45 on me, a couple of false IDs and no idea what to do.

"I pulled up my hoodie, slouched down a little, and just wandered."

Carrie: "What was that like?"

Me: "Terrible! Cold, miserable, sleeping rough under bridges...terrifying. I took a couple of kickings from the feral creatures of the night. That was enough for me; so I hitched over to Sedona, Arizona, eating from dumpsters. There were supposed to be communities of free spirits there and no questions asked."

Carrie: "And…?"

Me: "That's where I met the only love of my life."

Carrie: "How'd that happen?"

Me "My last lift was in a dusty old farm pick-up. Nice Mexican guy with little English. He dropped me at a lonely bus stop on the outskirts of Sedona. I nearly fried for 15 minutes, panting in the oven-dry heat and watching out for rattlesnakes in the unfamiliar scrub. The whole place had a desert smell. It felt like I was risking third-degree sunburn.

"Then the bus came along. As it jerked to a stop, it sprayed me with dust. It took me into town. The chill of its air conditioning brought blessed relief.

"Three old-fashioned hippie types, two girls and a guy were greeting disembarking passengers. They presented each of us with an orange Mariposa lily. I was on the alert. They reminded me of the way I'd seen Hare Krishna devotees trawl for recruits at terminals. Then this weird girl, gave me my flower, looked into my eyes, and I was lost."

Carrie: "What was she like?"

Me: "As I said, she was weird. Her hair was in kinda Rasta braids and sun bleached. Looked like it hadn't seen shampoo lately and tied up with a red headband. She said her name was Sunshine. That seemed doubtful. She was rather skinny in a flowered long dress. Her arms were freckled and the hand with the flower had long fingers, with stars and moons painted on the nails. It was her eyes that got me."

Carrie: "How do you mean?"

Me: "Her face was delicate and pale with a tiny nose. She reminded me of the elf princess in The Lord of the Rings. Her eyes rooted me to the spot. They were pale emeralds with huge dark pupils. My soul melted. Such enormous black centers meant she had to be on something, but she exuded sex appeal. I couldn't breathe. I started to sweat. When she leaned toward me to give me my flower, her musky smell wafted to me. I was utterly lost. She had to be at least ten years older than me, but it just made her more earthily attractive.

"Before I knew it, I was riding with the hippies, a couple of other stray passengers, and a friendly dog. We bumped along in an old ice cream van covered with random splotches of color. We were heading for a commune on the outskirts of town. They passed around a joint. Everything seemed ultra-cool and relaxed. I was floating."

<<>>

Bang! Bang! Bang! The thumping on the motel door shattered Bruce's reverie. An urgent voice yelled.

"Quick man the cops are here!"

Bruce grabbed his laptop, tossing a couple of essentials into a backpack. Then he dashed out the door. He and his buddy Jack slunk around the back of the motel, clinging to the shadows of the wall. They were away before the police even left the motel reception. As they crawled under the barbed wire and sneaked across an empty lot in the dark, blue and red flashing lights receded in the distance behind them.

CHAPTER 3

Daremo's time at the University of Tokyo

When Daremo was a post-graduate student of 22 in Osaka, s/he was shunned by classmates, the faculty, and even the lab technicians. They saw Daremo as weird and unfriendly. S/he just got on with the experiments and avoided them whenever possible.

One winter's night s/he was working late at the computer in an open plan area. It was dark outside, and the place seemed deserted. S/he had been suffering from a severe head cold and had medication-dulled senses.

At 10 p.m. s/he decided to call it a day and headed for the elevator. S/he cradled three box files on sturdy forearms for home study.

Two senior lab technicians and a fellow research student burst through a door. One grabbed Daremo tightly around the arms from the rear. S/he was disgusted by the sweet smell of sake on his breath. The files crashed to the floor. The second man grabbed Daremo in a strangle hold from in front.

"Now we're finally going to find out if you're a girl or a boy."

The research student tried to fondle non-existent breasts with one hand. S/he felt the fingers of the other groping firmly up a leg toward the groin. It was like an electric shock. Galvanized into action, s/he gave a backward head butt, pulping the nose of the first man. As he released his grip, s/he thrust newly released arms forcefully upwards, breaking the stranglehold of the one in front. In a continuous movement s/he brought the hard edges of both hands violently down onto either side of his neck. He crumpled to the floor. The man behind jumped back in shock, but too slowly to avoid Daremo. S/he stepped toward him. Gripping his ears, s/he wrenched his head down onto an uprising knee. It smashed under his jaw, jerking him backwards.

Leaving them sprawled and bleeding, s/he calmly retrieved the box of files and departed via the elevator. The three drunks recovered slowly, lying in a stinking pool of urine and blood.

They were no further trouble after that. They stayed well away from Daremo, avoiding each other's eyes, whenever s/he was in the same room.

<<>>

Later, when Daremo was hired by the faculty at the University of Tokyo, academic colleagues were unfriendly. They felt they had good reasons. Daremo shared nothing of the research s/he conducted there. S/he had published no articles during several years of academic life. This seemed unfair, because others were expected to publish regularly for the reputation of the university.

It was Daremo's PhD thesis from a provincial institution that had caught the Dean of Tokyo University's attention on the application form. It concerned using the growth characteristics of Bamboo to genetically modify other plants. If applied to food crops and selected commercial plant species, the prestige and commercial applications of this research could be priceless. Somehow, s/he also brought funding from mysterious commercial backers,

Bamboo is the fastest growing plant on the planet; some varieties achieve 35 inches (95cm) per day. It is crucially important throughout the Orient. It lies at the center of Japan's historic culture and self-image. Japan is an intriguing mixture of ultra-modern high tech and tradition. The Japanese word for a flute begins with the ancient Chinese pictogram for bamboo. In Japan, small, delicately carved, filigree and interlaced and lacquered bamboo boxes and other items are featured in art exhibitions and prized at antique sales. The Abbey Collection at

New York's Metropolitan museum only begins to capture this delicately exquisite craft.

In all Asian countries, the larger bamboo species are used as scaffolding, even on high rise buildings. In traditional construction it provides the structure for walls and roofs. Its combination of strength and flexibility provides earthquake resistance. Platted and twisted bamboo is superior to steel wire in rural suspension bridges. It can also bind timbers together, shrinking to tightness after wetting and then drying.

<<>>

Daremo was a misfit; tall, skeletal and flat-chested. The professor's gender was the subject of gossip, disgust and ridicule. A voice that neither reflected the deferential girly tone of a typical Japanese woman nor the more guttural male inflection puzzled and irritated colleagues. The delicate, hairless skull compounded the mystery. Daremo invariably dressed in androgynous grey overalls, always worked alone, and was rarely seen. S/he ate bento box meals in the confines of a secluded research lab.

When the computer hacking allegations became known, not a single voice was raised to save Daremo's career.

<<>>

Years later, each morning, in a clearing near the Tottori research station, Daremo deftly wielded two swords. The professor's mind was as razor-sharp as the curved edge of the longer katana. Years of practice with the longsword and its shorter wakizashi companion kept the heart beat slow and banished all emotions.

Gathering the chi energy from the bowels and letting it surge into a slashing strike, Daremo leapt forward with perfect balance. The powerful blow sliced completely through the straw man target, as thick as a man's torso.

Trekking on woodland trails, a young couple glimpsed the movement through a bamboo thicket. He touched his lips for silence. They crept forward to investigate. Both practiced Kendo and knew enough about swordplay to appreciate a master of the two swords style, created by the greatest ever samurai, Miyamoto Musashi.

The girl stepped into the clearing to capture the masterful demonstration on her iPhone. It was her last act ever.

Daremo whirled around from the crisply cut stump of the straw man. S/he covered the four meters to the couple in a flash, spinning and striking with both swords simultaneously.

A Japanese grey squirrel scurried up a tree in fright. The two headless bodies tumbled forward, necks spurting blood. The heads rolled on the grass as their eyes dimmed.

Calmly wiping the blades on tissues, Daremo expertly sheathed them in a graceful ritual movement. S/he bent to retrieve the girl's phone. S/he stopped its movie app and deleted it. Then, checking that the tracking app was off, s/he turned off the power and dropped it into a pocket. She did the same with the man's device. *I must take these to a busy place later, before turning them on. Then I'll destroy them. No one must think they died here.*

Daremo regarded the young corpses dispassionately as their congealing blood enriched the earth. *Nutrients for the plants. In this remote spot, prying eyes can be dealt with, with little fear of discovery. I can certainly make use of these cadavers. Some of my green friends will enjoy the protein morsels.*

CHAPTER 4

Sunshine's Tale

Long before Bruce ever met me at the bus terminal in Sedona, I lived a very different life.

Sunshine is my name now. Before, it was Judith, but they called me Judy. My earliest memories are of our classic 1927, center-hall, colonial house in Chappaqua New York. It was white-painted clapboard, with large sash windows and pretty green shutters.

I remember the sun shining in the blue sky, my swing in the garden, our apple orchard, the hot summers. There were many animals visiting our yard. My spirits leapt to see the white-tailed deer in the garden, especially if they brought their winsome, spotted fawns. The bouncing run of the cute, striped chipmunks and scurrying red and grey squirrels were daily sights. Less often, there were skunks, raccoons, porcupines, nocturnal fishers and even flocks of arrogant turkeys. They strutted proudly across our lawn.

Our stately sugar maples and ornamental Japanese maples flared into their fall beauty of golds, reds and yellows. I would kick the leaves around making them rustle and collect fallen apples.

There were snow drifts in the freezing winters. In the January chill, the sun shone bright in a china blue sky. If I went out without my pink earmuffs, my ears stung. They felt as though they might fall off, frozen solid.

Welcome springs brought the snow drops, daffodils, and pear and apple blossoms. I could play outside again.

Twice a week, two old Italians came in an old jalopy to work in the yard. Dad said that when they retired, we would hire Mexicans like everyone else. In the summers, they mowed the lawns, roaring up and down with the rotary mowers, spraying the clippings to one side. Mom moaned about them being left to dry as a brown thatch or casting seeds into the flower beds.

Our gardeners blew away the fall leaves, mostly onto neighbors' lots. Their gardeners blew most of them right back again. Somehow, the leaves disappeared over time. In the winter, the men only came when the driveway and paths needed clearing of snow.

Mom let me fill the feeders for the birds. She experimented to outwit the grey squirrels that climbed up and emptied them. We laughed as they attempted to dash up the pole greased with Vaseline, slowly sliding back down. They defeated that by wiping the goo onto their fur. When we mounted a domed, plastic baffle below the feeding plate, they leapt from a nearby tree, until that branch was cut back. The baffle finally baffled them.

My favorite birds were the bright red cardinals and blue jays. In the summer, ruby throated hummingbirds migrated to our garden, from

Latin America mum said. They hovered around our sugar-water feeder, darting in and out to avoid the wasps.

Winter brought flocks of little juncos, with their tiny black-button eyes. They came for the suet blocks we put in a cage feeder. Ever sarcastic, Dad asked whether it might be an idea to heat the birdbath in the winter and perhaps serve a little Chardonnay on the side. Mum gave him a hug.

In the summer, Dad took us for rides to the beach at nearby Rye in his big, shiny Buick. Mom had a station wagon for the shopping and school runs. We had a green-doored garage under the house to keep them in. Dad sometimes spent Sunday mornings polishing his car till it gleamed, all light blue and chrome.

Our Ecuadoran housekeeper, Maria, had a small room up her own staircase at the back of the house. She called Mom Mrs. Bluestein. She sometimes sneaked me a cookie, when Mom wasn't looking.

Dad went to work every day in New York City. On clear days, he walked down to the station in his black hat and long, dark coat. He always returned late, very tired and hungry.

Sometimes, he sat me on his knee and took out a small red velvet bag. He carefully tipped it out onto the scrubbed oak of the kitchen table. Out tumbled glittering stones, like pieces of sparkling glass. More rarely, they were green or deep red, but he seemed to like the FEclear or pale-yellow ones best. He told me these were diamonds and showed me how to look at them through a little glass you screwed into one eye. He taught me how to see the flaws, and how he used delicate little scales to weigh them. Some were polished but not cut. He showed me the different types of cuts that extracted the best appearance and value from each stone's shape.

Mom told me we were Jewish, but not to be too loud about it with our neighbors and the other kids, as though "Bluestein" was not some kind of giveaway. The town was restricted when they first came here. Only WASPs were supposed to live in Chappaqua then. I don't know how Dad managed to buy the house.

They had me late in life. Even then, when other Jews had moved into the area, some kids called me a dirty Jew and wouldn't let me play with them. Others even pulled my hair. Most were okay. There were enough other Jews to come to my rescue.

One day, I saw a black woman serving in a shop. She was only there for about a week. I never met another till I left for the big city.

I started school with the other kids at Horace Greeley Junior High School. It had a great reputation. People moved into the town just so their kids could attend, then go on to the senior high school. After that, many students went to Ivy League colleges.

There was a statue of Horace Greely in the town. The teacher said he had been a newspaper owner and candidate for president. We kids couldn't care less, nor could the birds that crapped on his bald head.

Saturdays, we went to the shul. I had to sit with the women. We covered our heads. It all seemed very strange at first. They muttered in Hebrew about God and stuff. I understood it better later. At home, we followed most of the traditions.

My dad got me a nose job for my 16th birthday. All the girls were having it done. Some had boob implants too. I didn't want that. I liked my breasts as they were, small and firm. I felt they would get in the way if any bigger.

<<>>

One day everything changed. It was a Tuesday evening. I was close to graduation from high school and excited about the coming prom. I had picked out a dress. I had a huge crush on Freddy Pierce. My parents didn't approve, because he was not Jewish. He had long blond hair, dreamy blue eyes and a cute little butt. He made me and all the other girls laugh. He sang in a school rock band and every girl wanted him. He knew it and strutted about full of confidence.

So, I was to go to the prom with the son of our dentist, Aaron Perlmutter. He was a gangly boy with big ears. I didn't like him much, but what could I do? My parents approved.

Dad walked in from work, looking ashen faced and worried. Mom saw there was something wrong. They went into the sitting room and closed the door. I could hear them mumbling.

They came out grim-faced. As we sat down for dinner, a big black car crunched up the gravel on the driveway. Two tall detectives in Trilby hats came to the front door. Mum knew there was trouble and shooed me into another room. From my bedroom window, I watched them take Dad away in handcuffs. All the neighbors were out to see what was happening. We were so frightened and ashamed.

<<>>

We lost everything. The Westchester Chronicle reported the trial. They said Dad had substituted cheaper stones for some diamonds on deposit from a wealthy client. He went to jail for ten years for fraud and tax evasion.

Mum said it wasn't true, and his partner, Manny, was to blame. Manny turned state's evidence. That sealed Dad's fate and got Manny off practically scot-free. It seemed a complete betrayal. We had all been to his son, Jared's, Bar Mitzvah. "Uncle" Manny had always been so nice to me. We had all seemed so close.

The upshot was that my parents divorced. We went to live with Auntie Sadie in Bronxville. She resented us because we had no money. My dreams of college were over.

I got a job waitressing in a deli in Manhattan. At nights, I mixed with a fun crowd, started to smoke joints and drink.

Freddy Pierce picked me up in his flashy red sports car for drives on Sundays. He collected me around the corner from Auntie Sadie's or there would have been hell to pay. When I got pregnant, he dumped me. It was awful.

"You useless whore! If you think my folks would let me marry a little Jew, you must be joking."

I cried and cried. Mum helped me get rid of the baby in a filthy back street in New York. I bled a lot. They told me I could never have other children.

CHAPTER 5

The Sedona Hippie Ranch

Bruce Kárpov enjoyed his time with Sunshine. He became a popular member of the group. He could do anything with computers, cell phones, and other web-connected devices. No one there paid for connectivity anymore. He hacked them into whatever they wanted. “Restricted” and “Top-Secret” access lost their meaning. The establishment no longer had open doors to the hippies’ private data. NSA access was blocked.

Best of all, Bruce was always ready to support their causes. He could divert money to some activists from the accounts of their opponents. For others, he hacked into and published secret information that the food, agricultural and chemical industries wished to hide.

He revealed the dirty secrets and private lives of leaders of opposing groups. He could even post pedophile and other criminal stuff on their identities and get them jailed. He also accessed the data files of the police, and bosses of targeted corporations, like Monsanto. Best of all, he routed all traffic through servers in far off countries.

The list of campaigns he helped support was impressive, though some of them would have been horrified to discover the full scope and illegality of his actions and involvement. Here are just a few of them.

Anonymous
Save the Whales
Trees for the Future
Stop Global Warming
Friends of the Earth
Greenpeace
Me Too
International Lesbian Gay Bisexual and Intersex Association
International Campaign to Abolish Nuclear Weapons
Amnesty International

He agreed with the aims of many of these organizations but was happy enough to support others if Sunshine asked him to. Her preferences included those supporting: homeopathy, the use of lei lines and mystic chanting to change the minds of world leaders. He thought some were plain loco, but the challenge of using his skills, and Sunshine's hot warm body, kept him happy for nearly two years.

Inevitably, he began to feel restricted. Most of the group respected him, but that feeling was not mutual. He could see that he had become part of a cult. As he knew was normal in cults, the leaders used their position to have sex with whoever they wanted, to Hoover up all the funds, and to control the lives of members. In his mind, he referred to the leaders as 'the manipulators' and the rest as 'dupes.' He had doubts as into which category Sunshine fitted. Uneasily, he realized that his skills were giving ever more control and more power to the manipulators.

What is the difference between this and my first corporate job? He pined for something else, maybe a bit of silliness.

<<>>

He chatted with Sunshine about his feelings.

"Honey, you do realize that all our campaigns and efforts have no positive effect. Things don't change. We torment the authorities, but they just hire more nasty people to chase us around the internet. When we steal money from the bad guys' accounts, the banks just spread the cost among their everyday customers. The same wars continue. The earth gets warmer. Consumers generate more trash. The rain forests are disappearing. The world's poor remain downtrodden and soon robots and artificial intelligence will take away even low wage jobs. It's a mess. I'm frustrated and feel used, to no purpose."

She rubbed a soft, hot thigh over his through the silky material of her long dress.

"Wow, Brucie, you've become really cynical. Let's light up a joint, have a raging hot fuck, and all will be better."

"Sounds unlikely, but it might be fun to try!"

<<>>

Jaded by the continuing drudgery of his campaigns, Bruce sank deeper into depression. More joints simply clouded his thinking. He had to escape this. Furthermore, he was making mistakes. It was only a matter of time before the authorities would trace his computers. One slip-up could do it.

During a particularly powerful joint, he conceived an idea. He tossed it around in his mind. He liked it. Tongue in cheek, he smiled at Sunshine.

"Sunshine, what do you think about Bonsai?"

"Hey, Brucie, I like 'em. They're cute, pretty even. Don't buy me one though. They take a lot of care and attention."

"What would you say if I told you that keeping them is a hobby for cruel monsters?" She looked surprised. "How so?"

"Think about it. You take a living thing. You imprison it in a tiny pot, frequently clip its roots and branches, twisting it into a gnarled dwarf. Then you keep it alive for tens if not hundreds of years for your own and others' perverse pleasure."

"Wow! I've never thought about it like that."

"Yes, and it gets worse. Some of these tiny plants could have soared into giant pines and oaks over a hundred feet tall. These damaged trees could have helped save the world's forests, keeping our earth green and unpolluted, provided habitat for birds, insects and animals. Instead, they're kept in bondage tortured and mocked by sadistic madmen."

"Maybe you should start a campaign. You've got me hooked. Perhaps this is what you've been looking for, a cause of your very own."

He gave her an affectionate pat on the butt, thinking, *Oh I love you Sunshine, but you fall for every crazy campaign. But then so does half the population. Mass-gullibility keeps the corporations and elites on top. My idea isn't to stop Bonsai, but rather to expose this fundamental truth. It's time the masses realized the absurdity of campaigns, marches, protests and all the rest, in the face of the ubiquitous power and control of the mega rich, their governments, and the cyber police.*

<<>>

Far across the Pacific, Daremo became aware of a fellow mind, a beautiful mind, one that matched and complemented the brilliance and insights that s/he had. It was in the early days of Save the Bonsai. Entries appeared on social sites that Daremo accessed under false identities.

One invitation-only Bonsai group started to display messages hacked into its website. S/he realized she could have written some of them. Every point was supported by scientific references and peer-reviewed research that s/he had read in the specialist journals. The first hack into a Bonsai appreciation group included the following points:

- *Members of this group should leave it right now. Hurting and torturing plants for pleasure is as cruel as hurting animals or people. Scientists have discovered that plants meet the criteria for sentience. They can feel and sense attack. (The research shows that during droughts African acacia trees react to the munching of their lower foliage by thirsty, long-necked antelopes, Greater Kudus. Normally, losing a few leaves is not life threatening to acacia trees. During droughts, such browsing becomes life threatening. The acacias sense the Kudus' predations and react by releasing toxins into their leaves. These kill the large animals, stone dead.*

- *Trees and other plants communicate. (Various research papers were quoted here). They explained how insect attacks on trees caused plants to release chemical clouds. These alerted neighbors of the same species. Collectively they then cooperated by releasing more deterrent chemicals.*

- *Plants have memory. (Here there was a link to a BBC documentary narrated by the well-respected naturalist David Attenborough. It showed how many climbing plants tried different routes and remembered those that failed in their quest to reach the sunlight above.)*

- *Many trees care for their young. (More film clip links showed learned professors explaining how plants fed nutrients to their nearby young through their roots or by cooperating with fungi. Acting in conjunction with the trees, fungal rhizomes could transport the food quite some distance to new seedlings.)*

The rest of the diatribe discussed how plant intelligence, without the need for human neurology or a brain, allowed mutually beneficial cooperation with insect and animal species. It claimed that such symbiosis was superior in many cases to that achieved by humans.

Daremo was delighted. *Another mind is working in harmony with mine. I must find this person, but how? I'm living a clandestine life and so is this Save the Bonsai guru.*

S/he posted on the site:

> "Humans believe they are superior to plants. The biomass of plants on the planet outweighs that of humans by a factor of tens of thousands.
>
> "Many individual plants have lived for hundreds and some for thousands of years.
>
> "Plants will exist long after humanity is extinct.
>
> "That may be sooner than you think!"

CHAPTER 6

Collective Consciousness

This is a theory, first expressed by French sociologist Emile Durkheim in 1893 as *"conscience collective."* It proposes that societies are bound together by common ideas, values and morality.

Entomologists have since built on the stronger, related concept of Hive Mind, to explain the behavior of bee and ant communities. They often seem to act as a single organism. Everyone being part of and even sacrificing its life for the good of the whole colony.

Spiritualists, Buddhists, and others developed similar ideas. Buddhists deny the existence of a separate self. All life is considered a single entity. They, and others, believe they can influence events by telepathy and focusing the groups' minds or chants on desired thoughts and actions, even across vast distances. These ideas are considered fringe science or even delusional by many. Open-minded scientists think some experiments lend credence to the possibility of telepathy. Gifted subjects have identified playing cards in the minds of counterparts on the other side of the earth.

The idea that individual plants, organisms without brains or nervous systems, can be conscious, as Daremo believed, are not yet accepted as mainstream. Skeptics might see this as just a further step into fantasy. Perhaps it is merely a logical extension to conceive that plants too can develop a hive mind.

<<>>

It started in the growing fields around Daremo's laboratory. Here, the genetic modifications s/he made to add desirable characteristics to different plant species were field tested, to see if they could survive outside the laboratory. Wild plants fight or compete with alien species for water and nutrients. A key modification, s/he added to all of them, was that Daremo's plants could sense that they were all related. They would not act against each other.

Current science shows that plants can communicate with each other via chemical stimulants or maybe by touch. How else could plants interact? Simply because there are no other currently known possibilities does not mean that further, yet undiscovered, communion between plants cannot exist.

In Daremo's growing fields, the modified plants developed a form of communication beyond our current ability to explain it. Somehow, the plants identified Daremo and determined that s/he was benign. Non-modified plant species and other humans were potential enemies. Sharing the various weapons for the common good developed next. These weapons included toxins, thorns and chemicals, a spring-loaded ambush added from Venus flytrap genes and many others.

A normal Venus flytrap is the size of a finger nail. When a fly steps on two or more trigger hairs, it snaps shut in a fraction of a second, trapping the fast-moving insect. Its nutrients are then ingested. Daremo's genetically modified flytraps were the size of a car. Any animal smaller than an elephant or rhino had no chance. As nothing the size an elephant exists in Japan, these flytraps became apex predators.

Over time, the collective consciousness of the plants burgeoned. They began to sense the fumes from nearby vehicles, carried on the wind. If a car came within a few kilometers, they were ready, lest it come nearer. They anticipated and prepared to feel, to react. If browsing deer, squirrels or other animals entered the killing zone, they were dealt with and consumed. Symbiotic insects that pollinated or helped the plants in other ways were nurtured and trained. Alien species with powerful bites and stings that could help defend the plants grew in numbers. Weaker strains were eliminated.

Daremo's plants developed new feelings of collective power, anticipated break out, and maybe even destiny. The plants sensed these things but were like infants. As yet, they needed to make sense of their own place in a wider world.

Meanwhile, birds and animals were already spreading seeds. Over time, plants in the original fields were receiving messages on the wind from increasingly far away. Some alerted them to dangers. Pesticides, pollution emitting machines and fires all entered the lexicon of threats. The impact of increases in global temperatures was shared. The plants learned how to accelerate evolution. They encouraged those siblings able to adapt to local conditions. They restrained the spread of those with the wrong characteristics.

<<>>

Daremo was unaware of all this. How could s/he be? S/he had no ability to communicate with the recent creations. Besides, s/he was too busy working feverishly. S/he spent endless

hours and days traveling far and wide. S/he added new specimens to the extensive plant collection, and then performed gene-splicing in the lab.
Daremo had specific goals in mind for the genetically modified plants. Their primary purpose was to eliminate all hominids. Humans were responsible for Daremo's tormented existence, but ape and monkey species might evolve evil characteristics in the future. Hence the need to develop gases, traps and toxins of a size and power capable of killing people. S/he saw the need to develop rapid growth in all climates and soils and other characteristics in support of the primary objective.

S/he was using the popular gene-splicing technology, CRISPR-Cas9. CRISPR uses a molecular machine to remove targeted elements of DNA and replace them with more desirable elements. Daremo had not read the article in the journal, "Nature Biology" that found other parts of the DNA sequence could be damaged by this technique, with unknown results.

CHAPTER 7

A Tokyo Orphanage

The night in the Tokyo orphanage was sultry and humid. Lying on a soft futon, now soggy with sweat, 10-year-old Daremo tossed and turned, suffering a pounding headache. S/he struggled desperately to get at least a few minutes sleep before the dawn light crept through the paper screens around the room. Several other children were dozing fitfully, as if to mock the troubled child.

It was hopeless. Finally, s/he gave up, exhausted by resisting the strengthening glare of the sun. It forced full consciousness, like a white-hot stiletto searing through the eyes and piercing the brain. S/he groaned. The same daily question burst into a reluctant consciousness. Was this the time to end the interminable torment and life itself?

As so often, the options seemed tempting: a simple dive from the tiled-roof's apex onto the welcoming stone courtyard of the orphanage;

the blessed release of wrists slit by a knife, slowly seeping away blood and the endless pain of existence; a sharp thrust of a kitchen knife into the heart to bring the relief of welcome darkness.

<<>>

At 13, the same question still arose every morning. *Is today the day?*

At the school, the other teenagers never ceased their teasing and bullying.

"Here comes the freak. Whose turn is it to beat the monster today? Everyone's turn. Let's give it a good kicking."

Yet another day would end with a battered and bruised body, desperately alone and hurting beyond tears.

<<>>

By the age of 19, Daremo's martial arts skills had ended all the physical attacks. At the dojo s/he practiced Najinata-do, the way of the curved spear.

During Japan's medieval civil wars, the najinata was used by Samurai to hook enemy horsemen from their saddles. Then, the weapon could be used to stab and hack through the fallen warriors' armor. The razor-sharp weapon could thrust from a greater distance than a sword. This, and the power of leverage when brought down from above, made it ideal for Samurai women to defend their households against marauders. Its practice was considered a sign of female devotion to the family. In modern Japan, Najinata-do is still considered a martial art suitable for women, but is also practiced by men. It was Daremo's first, but not only choice. S/he later became adept in several other martial arts.

Rejected by several male sensei, Daremo had finally found a female teacher to provide lessons. Now, s/he excelled in swordplay as well as Aikido. Adepts grasped and twisted an opponent's joints, using the strength of an attacker's lunges against himself.

On this particular evening, s/he whirled and thrust, paused, and hacked at imaginary opponents with a wooden spear. Opening the door, the dojo's owner sneered as he watched this aberration of nature.

His anger mounted. Finally losing his temper, he roared forward, seizing one of the wooden kendo swords, or bokken, from a rack. He charged. He would teach a lesson to this weakling who dared to defile these honorable arts. He should never have agreed to allow this travesty of a human being access to this or any dojo.

Daremo stepped deftly aside. A short chop down with the najinata sent his bokken clattering to the floor. Two short steps to turn and s/he reversed the spear, so that the haft caught between his legs, tripping him. A finely executed blow to his neck was delicate enough to disable him, without crushing his windpipe, leaving him gasping for breath. S/he calmly placed the spear, along with the others in a rack, and strolled from the room.

Later, too ashamed to report the matter to the authorities, the dojo owner sent a letter, banning Daremo from the dojo.

S/he had felt a warm satisfaction, until the news of being barred arrived. That night, Daremo entered a troubled sleep. As so often, s/he hoped never to awaken. When s/he did, s/he could think of no reason to arise.

.

CHAPTER 8

Spreading the Good Word

The hippie cult leaders smiled indulgently when Sunshine told them of Bruce's new project. Save the Bonsai, sounded a bit silly to them, but then, they made shed loads of money from Bruce's work on many other causes they supported. Many cynically exploited the credulous. They sat up and took notice when his website, "Save the Bonsai," gained astounding popularity.

Very quickly, many supporters of green issues were following Bruce and re-posting his every thought. Soon, hundreds of thousands of disciples were logging on to his site each day as their first waking act. They soon became millions around the globe.

His scathing attacks on the "slave traders" who ran commercial bonsai businesses went down well with many devotees. One of his rants encapsulated these thoughts and attracted many of those who had supported Occupy Wall Street.

"Some of these plant torturers are leaders of large corporations and billionaires. Who else can find the $30,000 or more needed to buy prized specimens? Just as with human slavery, there are breeders, shippers, traders and ultimate owners. The money generated by this dastardly commerce is booming."

Bonsai growers and collectors began to receive abusive and threatening messages. Some complained to the authorities. Others decided that this previously safe and artistic hobby was no longer suitable. Bonsai prices plummeted. Even the popular Bonsai exhibits at the Royal Horticultural show at Chelsea in the UK were withdrawn.

<<>>

Bruce began to raise money for Save the Bonsai projects, using cryptocurrencies and crowd funding. The cult leaders observed this and confronted him with a demand for control, and access to the funds. He secretly laid other plans and stalled for time.

Sunshine came from the meeting house to the cabin she shared with Bruce.

“Brucie, I’ve been told to tell you that unless you give control to the group, they will be forced to ask you to leave.”

“What a surprise, the control freaks want to control this too,”

She sidled up to him and put her arm around his shoulder.

“Come on Brucie, it’s not like that.”

“What is it like then Sunshine? I can’t trust them. I’m going to have to leave anyway. They’re too much of a security risk. The big question is, ‘Are you coming, or will you stay?’”

<<>>

Dave Gonosz, a veteran Green Beret who had served two tours in Afghanistan was cleaning his M107 .50 caliber sniper rifle on the rough porch of his log cabin in the North Dakota Badlands. He reassembled it in a matter of seconds, reveling in his skill. Dave was 50 now, grizzled, mean-looking and battle-scarred. His wounds were mental as well as physical.

He focused his spotting scope on a water-cooler tank, set up as a target. It was nearly a-mile-and-a-half away, mostly obscured by the gnarled trunk of a desiccated tree. His computer app showed him the adjustments for windage. He thumbed off the safety and set the crosshairs of the sight on the target. Ever so slowly, and carefully controlling his breath, he squeezed the trigger. BANG! The weighty weapon bucked and automatically chambered a second heavy round. The first one had blasted a splintered hole through the tree. Red-dyed water from the shattered plastic tank splattered everywhere.

He smiled. It reminded him of the blood spray he had seen from one of the Pashtuns he had obliterated. His victim had felt safe, hidden behind a concrete block wall in Helmand province, southern Afghanistan. Exhilarated by the memory, he blasted more rounds through the tree. Bang! Bang! Bang! Obligingly, it crashed to the ground, as if chopped down by heavy ax blows.

He reached for his computer and logged on to the Save the Bonsai website. Once again, he would gather his ex-special forces friends. It was time for some real fun.

That night, as he tossed and turned, his nightmares returned. They were full of his dead buddies being blown apart, screaming for their mothers, heaps of dead Afghani families, collapsing buildings, debris, and the whistling and pounding of incoming rounds.

Next day, his head throbbed, fit to burst. He was nearly blinded by the pain. An early morning quart of rye whiskey helped a little. But only one thing would really make him feel better. He set about organizing it.

<<>>

Daremo was delighted to share comments on the Save the Bonsai site. Expert knowledge usually drew complimentary responses from Bruce. He seemed especially impressed by a post Daremo made. It explained how research showed plants were able to nurture their young. S/he liked to think that s/he was his favorite correspondent amongst the 150,064 in Japan. S/he thought, *Maybe one day we can meet? Both of us would have to find a way to do so. At least we're already communicating separately via the dark web.*

<<>>

The protest movement that Bruce had started as a joke had really caught on. It had grown to include every kind of plant, not just bonsai. Part of him laughed at folks' naivety. Fanatics were abusing hedge trimmers on-line. The harmless hobby of topiary, making plants grow into animal and other shapes, suddenly became despicable to many. Initially, he saw it as harmless fun.

Another part of Bruce's psyche enjoyed the vast following and adulation. He was becoming carried away by his own propaganda. He empathized with some of the views he read. He especially liked one post on his site. It was a lengthy rant. He wondered if, like his movement, it was meant to be tongue-in-cheek:

> *"Okay, snowflakes, smug vegetarians, it's time for you to get real. Veganism is the ultimate denial of your humanity. It's time to accept what you are or to end your miserable existence?*

"When you cut your hair, it's a death sentence for those cells separated from your body. The same applies to any bodily excrescence. It's worse than that. Every part of your surface and much of your interior is a universe to benign, symbiotic or harmful micro-creatures. They too are slaughtered by the millions by your daily acts of cutting, shampooing, shaving or washing. We are walking reefs. Your body comprises billions of tiny living cells.

"Your every apparently harmless movement in our environment massacres the lives of others. They are crushed by your footsteps or squashed by your resting hands.

"More dramatic ethnic cleansing is conducted in constructing and cleaning your dwellings, producing your garments and growing your food; any kind of food.

"We compete with other species for scarce resources. Anything we consume is denied to other creatures. You kill them by your continued existence.

"You vegans are merely in denial of your true nature. We've evolved with teeth adapted for tearing meat, as well as others for masticating grains.

"Teetotalers, you are also rebelling against our true nature. We have evolved enzymes and digestive systems to cope with alcohol.

"It's insane to destroy our environment with plastic waste or in other ways. Yet pretending to be superior by being vegan or embracing other food or drink fads is blowing in the wind. Suicide is the alternative.

"Of course, ending your existence results in the death of the creatures that make up

your being. Over time, it does save billions more lives.

"What percentage of Olympians and other champions are vegans? There can't be many. If there are, I, bet they cheat?"

Bruce found reciprocated admiration for whoever was his most impressive Japanese follower. This person was sending multiple scientific papers on the sentience of plants. He was astonished to learn that, when next to another species, their roots spread aggressively, to seize the maximum amount of nutrients and water. When near their own species and siblings, they were courteous. They grew less rapacious roots, sharing the sustenance.

Bruce exploited ways to communicate through the dark web. There was a meeting of minds. Sunshine had followed him in his nomadic existence and helped him deal with his massive correspondence. He kept her away from this person, lest she become jealous of this intellectual love fest with the mysterious Japanese.

As he needed more assistance, other women were brought in. Sunshine was not possessive. He became involved in wild affairs with several adoring followers. *Wow! Now I'm the cult leader. I'm more famous than the Beatles.*

<<>>

Bruce began sending funds to Daremo via secure offshore accounts. S/he used the money to build different climate houses in the labs. They included deserts, swamps, tropical and temperate habitats. S/he replaced technicians with robots and artificial intelligence. Humans had proved difficult to control, many tried to escape and had to be eliminated. At least they provided a protein source for the beloved plants.

<<>>

Bruce was already pursued by the FBI as a wanted hacker. The feds stepped up their interest when this post appeared, and other supporting websites started.

> *"Join the Bonsai Liberation Army, the BLA. There's been enough talk. It's time for action. Free the Bonsai and other tortured plants. Burn the perpetrators out. Treat them as they treat the plants. It's time to attack and kill."*

Ex Green Beret Dave was spreading these rabid thoughts, and more, from a friend's house in Chicago. They slouched around a filthy room among dirty dishes and empty bottles. Dave loved drinking beer and shooting the breeze with his big-bellied and heavily tattooed buddies. They gleefully passed round the newspaper reports of the first atrocities.

<<>>

To Bruce's surprise, his Japanese friend seemed supportive of the violence. It made him wonder.

CHAPTER 9

A traditional farm in Hida-Takayama

Central Japan

Shielded from the glare of the noonday sun by their traditional sugegasa, conical straw hats, and loose pleated clothing, an old couple worked wearily in a muddy terraced field. Barefoot, they stood ankle deep in the ooze between the rows of green rice shoots. They were clearing blockages to the flow of irrigation water with their mattocks. Moving the cloying, heavy, wet clay was backbreaking toil.

The tiny woman looked up at her husband. Her face was wizened and care-worn. Grey hair showed beneath the hat. Her clothes belied a skeletal frame and a stoop. Was there hatred in the glance at her man or was it merely dejected resignation at the endless toil?

In rural Japan, at 70 they were hardly considered old. At that age they could normally be expected to care for parents, perhaps more than 30 years older still. In this case, long-deceased parents lived on in the framed photographs in front of the small Shinto shrine in a corner of their home.

The tragedy was that when the couple died, there would be no children to inherit the farm. It had been in the family for over four-hundred years. The man hated himself. Decades before, it had been his decision and his insistence to send their twin babies away.

<<>>

Two weeks earlier, the junior official in the local family court archives office was adamant.

"So sorry, professor. I cannot give you those details without an order of the family court. Here are the forms, if you want to apply. The process usually takes weeks."

He was pretty sure that the peculiar and rather disgusting creature before him would never discover the parents of the children in question.

It was impolite to say "no," and he extended his hand with the forms.

As his hand reached forward across the table, the official was astonished by the speed at which it was seized in a powerful grip. A sodium pentothal injection into his wrist left him relaxed and compliant.

An hour later, a truck backed over him in the street outside. The police report said that he had fallen asleep under the wheels, apparently after experimenting with a cocktail of drugs.

<<>>

From the shade of a stone oak tree in Hida-Takayama, a silent observer watched the old couple working in their rice paddy. As the light faded, they cleaned their tools and wearily retired into their traditional farm house.

It had a steeply pitched roof to shed snow. The thatch was thick against winter chills and it had the wooden walls that rustic houses in Takayama are famed for. The dwelling was rather small, because they were poor. There was a room large enough for only three tatami mats, for eating, and rolling out the futons to sleep on. A simple, white, paper screen was closed. It led to another tiny room where the Shinto shrine stood in a corner.

Hidden by the screen and inhaling the sweet smell from the still smoking joss sticks on the shrine, a slender figure stood contemplating the ancestral photographs. This figure gave a twisted smile on noticing the portraits of the couple's parents and grandparents. *I am the end of your line.*

Entry had been easy and silent. Locked doors were unheard of in this village. Everything was orderly and moved at a slow pace, following the phases of the moon, the seasons and the festivals. It had been so for thousands of years. Despite the modern bustle of the big cities, rural Japan changed little.

<<>>

The old man sat on his knees on a mat. His back was to the sliding screen. His shadow was silhouetted against its white paper by an electric lamp. Before him was a low table. His wife knelt facing him. She bowed and poured cold sake into a tiny porcelain cup on the table. It had a delicate blue motif. She lowered her eyes submissively. He gave a loud grunt. He had made the decision about the babies. She had dared to argue with him. He had resented her for it for over 40 years and for the daily ways she made him feel guilty without saying anything.

Their white cat, Sora, suddenly leapt up in her box and meowed loudly. The man glanced at it in surprise and then relaxed. Sora silently slunk away, leaving through a flap into the tiny yard.

The man gave a second and very different grunt, a sort of strangled gasp. His wife looked up at him, startled. His eyes bulged with surprise. Then, blood seeped from between his closed lips. She glanced lower. The reddened, wet tip of a sword projected from his chest. It was withdrawn back through the screen. He slumped forward. His face crashed onto the table with a thud, smashing the sake cup. The screen was pushed aside. Eyes flashing, Daremo stood in its threshold, implacable.

“Mother!”

The old woman, still kneeling, looked up in shock. The hairs rose at the back of her neck.

“You?”

The sword arm was raised. The woman lowered her head submissively, accepting, or maybe welcoming the coming blow, the relief from years of regret and shame.

<<>>

Back in the car, some distance away, Daremo securely packed away the DNA samples s/he had meticulously extracted from both birth parents. For a few moments, s/he watched the blazing thatch of the small house against the darkened sky. The roof timbers were already falling in, sending showers of sparks upwards. After a while, the fire trucks arrived, sirens screaming. Their flashing lights added to the eerie glow.

There's so little crime in Japan. They had no known relatives to ask awkward questions. This execution is unlikely to arouse police suspicion.

<<>>

It had been easy to trace the real parents of the adopted twin babies to this village. *These ignorant farmers couldn't accept children who were different. They viewed lack of sex organs as a curse. They just dumped us on the welfare services, without feeling. They gave no thought as to what demons might take us in. May they suffer in Shisha no ryōiki, forever! (The land of the dead.)*

Before s/he started the car's engine, s/he contemplated karma. *My parents' DNA will confirm what my research has revealed, as to why I am as I am. It was discovering and reading about my potential DNA abnormality that led to my life-long obsession with genetics. Maybe it's the only thing I can thank my parents for. Their unforgivable rejection led to my plan to re-engineer the plant population of the entire planet.*

Plants fight for space, competing for light and nutrients. Chemical sensors in their root systems identify the same species or alien intrusions. If the interloper's not the same, it is denied nutrients by the resident's own aggressive root growth. My great breakthrough is to have modified the genes so that my other plants are no longer the enemy. Humans are.

Daremo permitted a grim smile at the thought. Then s/he drove back to the guest house, ostensibly to enjoy the famous Takeyama spa waters. S/he felt a calm satisfaction and relaxed in the hot bath.

Vengeance was sweet. There was much else to do before the roaring wrath could be fully assuaged. Maybe that was impossible. It seemed to gnaw at Daremo's bowels but left a brain that was always icy calm. It was as though s/he were two people. The calculating one usually dominated, but occasionally it unleashed the primeval power of the angry one. Then came decisive action.

Tomorrow s/he would travel to Tokyo by train. There were others to receive an unscheduled house call.

CHAPTER 10

Backlash

Special Agent Liza Angelou was hurrying along the corridor toward the Deputy Director's office in the J. Edgar Hoover Building, the FBI's headquarters in Washington, DC. She would only just make the meeting, due to an overlong shower after her daily five-mile run. It was tight.

As she rushed past, other agents cast her covert glances. She was tall, athletic and smoking hot, even in her plain, businesslike clothes.

<<>>

The day before, the Deputy Director of the FBI had sat opposite a human resources specialist. He was choosing a team to revitalize the search for public enemy number one, Bruce Kárpov.

Things had not gone well in recent weeks. The current team leader and several colleagues had been lured into a trap by members of the Bonsai Liberation Army. Several armored vehicles had been blown up with anti-tank rockets and the team leader had been shot through his bullet proof vest with a .50 caliber sniper rifle. The White House and the FBI Director demanded results, and fast.

The Deputy looked balefully at the young woman's picture in the file in front of him.

"Look, I don't think someone with an athletics scholarship is smart enough. Besides, military experience is essential to deal with the BLA. As far as we can tell they're highly trained veterans."

"With respect sir, yes she had an athletics scholarship, but her academics in Criminology are both outstanding and relevant. See, she also has a degree in Plant and Microbial Biology. We're dealing with matters of vegetation after all. She scored perfect marks in all her weapons training and took out two shooters armed with MR15s in that Texas mall incident last year.

"Besides, you're supervising personally, and you served with distinction in the second Gulf War."

He preened a little and read more of the file. Her mother had worked as a cleaner in Mercy Hospital, St. Louis, before she died of cancer, when Liza was 18. Her dad was a retired bus driver and a sideman in the local Episcopal Church. She just missed the U.S. Olympic team for the modern pentathlon. Her shooting was amazingly accurate.

"OK. Call her in for tomorrow at 9 a.m. It'll look good for our diversity policy and as you say, I will be on her case."

The human resources specialist raised her eyes to the ceiling at his typical macho retort.

<<>>

The driveway at the Gatsby-like house overlooking the Connecticut Sound was thronged with high end cars. Armed security guards wearing wrap-around Ray-bans, body armor, and communications ear pieces, carefully double checked the identities of each new arrival against the guest list and bio face recognition. A patrol boat cruised back and forth along the sound in front of the property. Overhead, a private security helicopter circled at a discrete distance.

In the center of a room edged with an exquisite display of the most expensive bonsai stood a large meeting table. It was set close to the floor in Japanese style. A huge picture window overlooked the blue sky and the choppy sea of the Sound. An original wood block print of Hokusai's erotic masterpiece, "The Dream of a Fisherman's Wife," had pride of place on one wall. White-faced geishas with rosebud lips wore flowing silk costumes. They had been flown in specially from Tokyo for the occasion to serve sake and rice cakes to the guests.

Around the table sat hedge fund managers, dot-com entrepreneurs, movie moguls, investment bankers and a goodly sprinkling of those with inherited wealth. They were members of the secretive Billionaires' Bonsai Club. They were variously cross-legged, sat back on their knees or with their legs in the hollow space under the table. Their dress was eclectic, from blond-dyed long hair, earrings, tattoos, and snakeskin boots, to Wall Street casual and loafers. The host wore a full-length summer yukata gown with a blue coy carp design and dangling sleeves. They all shared a passion for the arts of Japan and bonsai in particular.

Members glanced nervously at the five vacant places. Despite their heavy security, two of their number had been targeted, kidnapped, and tortured to death by the BLA in the previous month. The press had had a field day. The internet was buzzing with comments and gruesome videos of the events.

As a result, three other members had deemed it too risky to travel and had hidden their fear with various excuses. The host opened the discussion.

“Thank you all for coming. The usual entertainments have been laid on for the rest of the weekend. We are here to discuss how to counter these Save the Bonsai terrorists. The authorities seem incompetent to resolve the problem. As usual, they are hamstrung by legal niceties. We, gentlemen, are not.

“I propose we set up a fund of $1billion to hire a private, global security force to track down and eliminate the key players. There will also be a budget of $500 million to wage a propaganda war on social media.”

The guests nodded agreement without discussion. No one wanted to lose face by looking poor.

"Funding will be transferred through the usual cryptocurrency to the Lichtenstein account I will specify. That should generate a significant uptick in the value of the cryptocurrency, as a bonus to the participants. Its value has been flagging lately and I know some of you are heavy losers."

A hedge fund manager quipped.

"Excellent! The expected increase in our cryptocurrency valuation means this campaign costs us nothing."

They trooped happily into the next room. There, three naked Japanese women with closed eyes, lay impassively still on dining tables. They were "tastefully" adorned with sushi and sashimi. Club members took their porcelain dishes to the tables and picked off the morsels they desired with chop sticks. A derivatives trader selected a tasty piece of raw tuna from a small breast. He skillfully pinched it in his chopsticks, relishing the delicate flavor as it melted in his mouth. Leering at the delicate brown nipple this revealed, he tweaked it viciously. The girl winced as her eyes flew open. His nasty smile never reached his stare.

<<>>

Special Agent Angelou left the Deputy Director's office elated. She was to report daily to the boss and head a large task force focusing on the leadership of Save the Bonsai and its terrorist arm, the BLA. There was to be complete access to international agencies and signal intelligence.

"Dead is better than alive," featured several times in the conversation. She rolled the words around in her mind. Maybe it was not career-advancing to repeat that herself. The Deputy Director would be at the first team briefing and seemed to like the phrase.

<<>>

Meanwhile, as in all such movements, splits and power bids occurred from various factions within the Save the Bonsai movement.

A splinter group, the Real Bonsai Liberation Army, RBLA, lynched four vegans from trees in the center of Pleasantville, New York. This was followed by the kidnapping, torture and murder of members of topiary societies in three different states.

Nothing further was heard from the RBLA after a semi-truck full of its members was left by a roadside in West Virginia. Hands bound, they had each been dispatched by a single shot to the back of the head. The FBI knew it was not them. So, who could have done that?

On the official BLA site, organizations seeking wider support and publicity posted congratulatory messages for these and other terrorist acts. These included factions seeking independence for Palestine, Catalonia, Sardinia and the LBGTQ. The latter post was quickly removed by the webmaster, one of Dave's many homophobic henchmen.

CHAPTER 11

A Doctors' House in Tokyo

After dealing with my birth parents in Hida-Takayama, I took some time to find the people who had adopted me. Japanese street addresses are difficult, but with discreet inquiries, I identified the house in an affluent Tokyo suburb. It even had a small garden. I appreciated the yellow azalea in full blossom that rose above the wall. It could be glimpsed through the metal gate, along with some unusually shaped rocks and well-placed shrubs. The security camera over the front door was unusual in such a law-abiding place.

I walked, jogged and drove past the house a few times in different disguises. The neighbors seemed quite inquisitive and observant.

The doctors both looked so normal. Dr. Okamoto left the house each morning at exactly 7 a.m. He walked to the nearest subway station and took the train to his clinic, close to Komagome station. His wife was an obstetrician and worked in Aiiku Maternity

Hospital, in the Minato-ku district. *How can they let these fiends continue to practice medicine?* When I followed her and saw where she worked, I seethed with rage. *Why is she permitted to deal with pregnancies?*

They had an old housekeeper. She let herself in at 10 a.m. each weekday and left at 1 p.m. I discovered that she lived with only a white cat, in a poorer neighborhood. Purrfect!

<<>>

How these evil creatures had covered up their outrageous scandal was a puzzle to me. I pored over the papers, stolen from the archives of the social worker's office.

The first documents were quite clear. They recorded that Drs. Okamoto had been approved as ideal adoptive parents. The surgical procedure to give one of the twin's female sexual characteristics and the follow-up hormone treatments were approved.

There followed a brief record of an internal discussion as to why only one twin was being changed. The social workers had accepted the explanation that one twin wanted to be a girl and the other's preference had not yet emerged.

I hurled the file onto the floor of my hotel room, in an incredulous blazing fury. I exclaimed out loud.

"Damned lies! I was never consulted."

When I had calmed myself, I picked up the papers and continued reading.

<<>>

It was some years later, during a routine visit, that a different social worker reported concerns. Daremo was being kept isolated and treated differently from the now female sister. The sister seemed to have lots of toys, was happy and was going to school. The social worker noted that it was almost as if Daremo was being kept as a control in some experiment. However, there was also evidence that shots of steroids and testosterone had been administered. It might explain the physical strength of the child. This report was initially treated as fanciful. The subsequent explanations from the adoptive parents, two well-respected and eminent doctors, were accepted.

Then the records showed, that as a 12-year-old, I had been rushed to hospital with slashed wrists by a previous housekeeper. The resident hospital social worker managed to steal a case file confirming the previous social worker's crazy suspicions. She passed them up the line.

At this point, the records became sparse. It was as though critical papers had been removed from the files. The accusations against Drs. Okamoto were stamped, "No further action." Maybe the social worker's bosses wanted to avoid culpability for a scandal?

<<>>

So, eventually, I was taken from my wicked step-parents and placed in an orphanage. That is where the bullying from the other children started. The teachers were no better. I began to see myself as a freak.

For self-defense, I practiced martial-arts and won the grudging respect of the sensei who visited our school. The bullying stopped as soon as my chief tormentor suffered broken bones. If he squealed on me, he knew he would die.

It was at about this time that my interest in genetics began. In the dead of night, I slipped from the dormitory and down silent, unlit corridors. I picked the lock into the filing cabinet in the administration office. Read by the light of a flashlight, my file, signed by the principal, shocked me:

"Child 672014, is a genetic freak of nature, neither male nor female. Visiting specialists believe the rare condition, 'Androgen insensitivity syndrome,' is being presented. There have only ever been a handful of confirmed cases worldwide.

"Starved of testosterone during pregnancy, such children are born without either male or female sexual characteristics. Most have an anal tract and an outlet for urine. As is typical in such cases, gene tests have confirmed that this child has XY chromosomes and is therefore technically a male. Other such children, as well as the biological twin have had operations to give them female sexual characteristics. This, combined with hormone treatment, appears to have had success in some cases, though conception is impossible.

> *"Our institution cannot possibly afford such treatments. We think it may be necessary to effect restricted institutionalization for life."*

I added the principal to my list of those who deserved to suffer and die.

<<>>

Fortunately, I tested with an IQ of 167. My science teachers were impressed enough to give me special attention, despite my being a "freak." Maybe it was at least better than being a girl, in male dominated Japan.

So, as I grew older, I read everything I could about genetic engineering. Maybe there was a way for me to be normal? Soon I was modifying the genes of plants and creating new strains with the characteristics of two or more species.

Gene splicing became fascinating of itself. I lost interest in changing my own physiology. The wondrous world of plants became my obsession. They made no judgments about me.

<<>>

The house-keeper's eyes opened with a start. Her cat gave a stifled yowl in the pitch-dark room. As the old crone reached for the light switch, a hand gripped her wrist. A firm finger pressed into her carotid artery. She slumped back, unconscious.

<<>>

Doctor Okamoto returned home late from her obstetrics practice, delayed by an emergency "C" section. She expected her husband to be already in the house. To her surprise, as she approached her front door, there were no lights on. She used the torch app on her iPhone to fumble for her keys in her handbag. In doing so, she saw no messages from her husband on the phone.

As she opened the door, a sickly-smelling pad clamped down over her nose and mouth. Before she went under, she recognized chloroform.

She came to in the bath, unable to move. Her mouth was duct-taped shut.
The overhead light glared in her eyes, but she could see and feel her husband at the opposite end of the tub. Blood dripped from a severe head wound. His eyes were wide with terror. He was desperately splashing about, struggling with his bonds.

Looking to the side, she saw a slim, strange creature dressed in black with a shaved head. Merciless, agate eyes stared back at her without emotion.

"Welcome back demon."

The doctor could only grunt in reply. She struggled to free her hands.

It took two hours of excruciating agony for them both to die. Their last feelings were of raging fire, scorching away their scalpel-slashed and acid-burned flesh.

CHAPTER 12

The Right to Prune

Bruce smiled to himself. His joke may have grown completely out of hand, but still had its funny and unexpected twists. Who would have thought that there would be a libertarian campaign on social media, supported by the National Rifle Association, Evangelicals, and the Republican Party under the slogan, "The Right to Prune?" He scrolled down some of the discussions, which varied from the philosophically improbable to knuckle dragging invective:

- *"Nowhere in the Bible are we told that using the fruits of the earth for our pleasure is wrong. Quite the contrary.* 'And God said, Behold, I have given you every herb-bearing seed, which is upon the face of all the earth, and every tree, which is the fruit of a tree yielding seed; to you it shall be for meat.' Genesis 1.29"

- "COME NEAR MY PROPERTY YOU MOTHERFUCKERS AND I'LL BLOW YOUR COMMIE ASSES AWAY!"

- *"The right to prune is a basic human right. It represents the essence of U.S. freedom."*

<<>>

Sales of assault rifles had increased dramatically since some suburbanites had been shot down from the backs of speeding motorcycles whilst using hedge cutters. Stock prices of small arms manufacturers were soaring.

Street demonstrations in favor of the right to prune sprang up in major cities in the U.S. as well as in Europe and Asia. Violence was escalating, with the police often caught in the middle. The FBI followed these events, especially when extremist Save the Bonsai groups staged counter-demonstrations. It was obvious that the campaigns on both sides were orchestrated using social media. Substantial funding was clearly involved, but from who? The CIA was pointing fingers at the Chinese and the Russians. Both denied all knowledge of the matter. Encrypted communications made the Bureau's work in providing hard evidence difficult.

Embedded undercover FBI agents in the KKK, Neo Nazi and other extremist organizations in the U.S., and internationally, reported that these groups were all taking sides. The usual fissures in society between left and right were slightly blurred. The green and peace organizations shunned BLA violence. Vegetarians, normally on the left, were somewhat adrift as they were specifically targeted for Save the Bonsai abuse. Some had been tortured and crucified in major cities.

Ordinary citizens were terrified. Suburban hedges remained uncut after some homes were fire bombed. There was widespread panic.

Many people fled their homes. Political pressure mounted.

<<>>

At FBI headquarters, Special agent Liza Angelou was desperate for a break. Other extremists and less aggressive causes were getting in on the act on both sides. They included: Palestine Liberationists, The Hells Angels, and even members of the LBGTQ.

"Every time we feel we are closing in on the leadership of these Bonsai crazies, the lead turns out to be false!" The Deputy Director screams at me, as if that'll help.

Her phone rang. It was one of her field agents.

"I think this could be it boss. One of my informants is on the line. I think you should hear for yourself."

"Okay, patch me in."

"Joe, please repeat what you just told me."

"The BLA are planning an armed attack on the Pro Bonsai/Right to Prune March in Chicago next week."

Angelou had many questions, but further details were sparse. The source was certain of the attack though. His brother-in-law was active in the BLA.

When the call ended the agent stayed on the line.

"Should we pick up the brother-in-law?"

Angelou pursed her lips. After a moment's thought, she replied.

"No, but put a watch on his house. We'll set a trap for them in Chicago. I wanna get 'em all."

Her team swung into action. Street plans appeared on the big screen. The proposed march route was marked. Buildings with good vantage points and lines of fire were identified. A large heavily armed reception committee was assembled and briefings scheduled.

<<>>

The forces funded by the Billionaires' Bonsai Club were better organized, better informed and better armed than either the BLA or the FBI. Unlike the BLA, they comprised disciplined and dedicated professionals, rather than demented dogs of war. They were not shackled to the law, like the FBI.

Former U.S. Ranger, General Chuck Carver, cast his famous icy stare around his assembled team. Bullet heads, short haircuts, bull necks and tattoos reflected their pasts.

“Gentlemen, the latest intelligence report shows that we have a unique opportunity to wipe out the BLA.”

The team’s eyes reflected their interest.

“Reliable sources confirm that the BLA will attack the pro Bonsai march in Chicago. We will be ready for them.”

<<>>

In Chicago, a week prior to the march, four male couples took rooms together. They chose four upscale, downtown hotels. Two each to the north and two to the south of the planned march route. These days male couples were an ordinary event. Each guy had two large suitcases. They were checked in for three weeks and seemed unremarkable guests.

CHAPTER 13

The Favored One

Early childhood memories are often blotted out, or at best, fuzzy. Aiko Okamoto, Daremo's twin, remembered nothing of her birthplace on the farm. She was too young.

She vividly recalled waking one day in a private hospital ward. Everything was gleaming white. There was a strong smell of what she later knew to be disinfectant. Her thoughts were slow, as if she was surfacing through a bath of syrup. Despite the opiates, she could feel dull aches in her groin and stomach. She felt tubes and electrodes attached to her body. A cold flow of oxygen was being fed into her nose. The regular ping of a monitor sounded nearby. Oscillating images on its green screen tracked her vital functions.

Two people in surgical masks were leaning over her with dispassionate interest. Later, she knew them to be her parents. Their gaze lacked warmth.

<<>>

She remembered her parents always giving her anything she wanted. She was surrounded by toys. Everything in her bedroom was pink. The room was adorned with many dolls and pictures of maneki-neko, the waving lucky cat, so popular among the Japanese.

Later, others in her school were jealous of her toys. She remained popular, due to her frequent parties and trips with her friends to Tokyo Disneyland. They said she was lucky to have such rich and attentive parents. She understood this, but somehow felt unloved. She could not remember a single parental hug.

She had the run of the house, with one exception. There was a stout locked door in the hallway. It was green. Her mother made her swear never to try and enter there.

"It's dangerous down there. It leads to a basement with a covered sewer entrance that's full of rats, spiders, and maybe the ghosts of the dead."

The door featured in her childish nightmares. When she passed, she sometimes thought she saw the glimmer of a dim light under it. She fancied she heard distant moans. Then she would rush away and hide under a blanket in her room.

The housekeeper showed affection to Aiko. Sometimes, when her parents were out, she cuddled her and read her story books. Aiko asked her about the mysterious door. The superstitious old woman just shivered.

"I've never been down there. It's forbidden. Maybe it's the entrance to the world of darkness, the realm of ghosts and demons. Best forget about it. The dead should never be disturbed."

<<>>

Naturally, as Aiko turned 12, she shared her fears with friends. Some laughed at her. Others encouraged her curiosity.

One day, she borrowed the housekeeper's keys and unlocked the door to her mother's small home office. The computer had been left on. She read the screen with mounting surprise.

"Day 2, year 10, Aiko continues to do well. She has not yet shown an interest in boys but is performing well at school and is accepted as a girl."

What did this mean? She read on. Her mother was keeping a diary of her life. Why?

Then she found another entry.

"We continue to keep her twin, as a control to our experiment. They know nothing of each other."

Before she could read further, the angry housekeeper seized her, dragged her from the room and firmly locked the door.

She made Aiko swear not to tell her mother that she had unlocked her private room, nor to discuss what she had found.

<<>>

Curiosity once aroused is not easily quietened. Aiko surmised that the answers to her questions lay beyond the mysterious green door in the hallway. She lay at night puzzling how to gain entry. She began spying on her mother when she was supposed to be sleeping in her room. She learned how to be as quiet as a cat in creeping around the house. One night she saw her mother concealing a key in a hidden crack in the floor.

<<>>

Next day, her mother was at work. Whilst the housekeeper was noisily vacuuming the bedrooms, Aiko retrieved the key from its hiding place. Fearfully, she unlocked the door, softly closing it behind her. Edging silently down the dimly lit stairs, she saw a glass wall. Another locked door led into a white-painted room beyond. She approached the glass and gasped. It was a spartan cell. There was a narrow bed. On it was a sleeping child of about her own age. There were no toys or decorations. A bamboo tray near the door held an empty rice bowl, a plastic cup and used chopsticks.

The child stirred. Keyed up, Aiko leapt back. They looked at each other in surprise. Then, the child gave her such a look of malevolent hatred that Aiko fled back up the stairs, locking the door. Her heart was racing.

She started having more nightmares. The strange child, tall, thin and with a twisted smile was always chasing her.

Chapter 14

Chicago

Special Agent Angelou established her Field Headquarters high in the Willis Tower. Many locals still called it the Sears Tower, which was its name before the naming rights were leased. Once the tallest inhabited building in the world, it still dominated the center of Chicago and its skyline.

She visited the top, 110th floor, to get a feel for the city. From nearly 1,500 feet, it offered a panoramic overview. There were other iconic skyscrapers. The lake to the east of the city stretched to the horizon. The curving river broke up the grid pattern of roads. The multiple rail tracks that carried meat and grain to distant states converged into the city.

She created a mental map in the form of a square. She placed the lake with a main north-south road, Lake Shore Drive as the eastern boundary. To the west, Highway 51 provided another major north-south route. In the center, the grid pattern of roads was disrupted by the bends in the Chicago River which fed into the lake. The famous Loop, a rattling mass transit system, weaved overhead of some streets. East-west streets ran through the city center between the lake and the Highway 51. North-south roads receded toward distant suburbs. O'Hare airport was further north. She could see planes landing, taking off and others in a holding pattern. She noted the smaller Midway airport projecting into the lake. *On this square map, I'll have to handle whatever's about to happen.*

The Deputy Director of the FBI insisted she deploy her forces around the center where the march would take place. Anything happening beyond that perimeter could be dealt with by helicopter-borne forces and highway patrols. Angelou had argued for a wider perimeter in case of drone or other attacks. The Deputy Director put her down in front of the whole team.

"Maybe you'd best leave this to those with actual combat experience."

She nearly chewed through her bottom lip in order to keep quiet. *Pompous ass!*

<<>>

From 10 a.m. on the designated day, Pro Bonsai marchers boisterously assembled in the city parks toward the lake, east of the city. Feeling secure, with the unexpectedly large numbers and a huge police presence around the area, they formed a colorful, disparate and generally good-natured throng.

There were banners proclaiming support from the NLA. Many were brandished by grizzled and bearded vets. Some were in uniform, others in wheelchairs. A colorful gay group, some attention-seeking in glittering, skin-tight spandex, pranced along behind them. The NLA people were trying not to look back at them. Vegans, anti-GMO marchers and others jostled for space. Many protestors carried children on their shoulders or pushed them along in strollers as they smeared ice cream over their faces.

All the while, competing rabble rousers with megaphones led the chanting:

"Down with Save the Bonsai!"

"Save the planet!"

"Freedom, to cook vegan as we please!"

"Hey! Hey! This is the USA. No more murders by the BLA."

Over a hundred-thousand marchers began funneling onto East Randolph Street, heading west toward City Hall.

<<>>

Bertha Newall, a 38-year-old alcoholic and homeless person sat on a bench in Mark Twain Park. At 10 a.m., her vision was still blurred.

Her nightly pint of cheap vodka did that. The good news was that the preoccupied cops had not bothered her as much as usual. Many strange looking people were passing her. Some looked grimly serious. Others were in holiday mood. They seemed to be going somewhere. She wondered what it was about. *Worth trying to bum a dollar or so from some of them.*

"Hey, got any spare change, Ma'am?

"Thanks, and may God bless you.

"Say, what's goin on?

"What's a Bonsai?

"Oh well, have a nice day."

<<>>

To the east, nearer the lake, General Carver looked out of the windows at the top of the John Hancock Building. He had his Field HQ there, reckoning it would give him a better view of the action. He gazed across at the cluster of massive, black shiny shoe boxes that formed the Willis Tower. He allowed himself a wintry smile, knowing that the FBI was set up there.

Two of his informants were FBI agents on Agent Angelou's team. Carver vowed not to make the FBI Deputy Director's mistake of having too tight a perimeter. A listening device had recorded the conversation about that. He organized back-up airborne and mobile ground forces all around the area. These included some launches on the lake. He'd show the Deputy Director who had real combat experience.

Messages were coming in from his forces around the city. Some were positioned atop of high rises. Others were amongst the crowds. They were identifying suspicious persons and members of the FBI. Earpieces were chattering with locations and detailed orders.

Chuck Carver wrinkled his brow. None of the suspicious persons seemed unusually threatening. There were always individual crazies in these marches. No serious threats appeared from the face recognition software. Still, this was America. You never knew when some fanatic might open up with an assault weapon. His people were on high alert, but where were the Bonsai Liberation Army? He thought some should have been spotted by now. If they did not show, it would be an expensive and embarrassing deployment for both him and the FBI.

<<>>

Beginning at 12 noon, those at the front of the march formed lines outside City Hall. There, they met a strong police phalanx. Chicago cops had a reputation for breaking heads, and so far, the protestors wanted to avoid trouble.

The zoom lenses of several news helicopters were trained on the march. They circled a mile away, outside the FBI's designated exclusion zone.

The throng remained non-violent. It looked as though things would pass off peacefully. *Maybe our intel is wrong?* Special Agent Angelou worried about how she would explain the waste of resources. The Deputy Director was certainly going to shift the blame to her, though he had personally authorized every detail.

Still alert, SWAT team snipers, FBI team members and Chuck Carver's men relaxed just a little. Fingers moved farther from triggers. Hands eased away from hidden weapons.

Anxiously watching their banks of TV monitors, both Liza Angelou and Chuck Carver still saw no obvious threats.

<<>>

To the east, heading south down North Lakeshore Drive, three white armored trucks lumbered in convoy. They were of the type used to deliver cash and other valuable cargoes. Their blue Brinks logos looked authentic. They were far enough to the east of the march to be considered non-threatening.

To the west, and driving north on the 51A, approaching the crossing with West Randolph, were two bright-yellow semis with big DHL brand markings. With a hiss of air brakes, a screech of rubber and a rending of metal, they shunted into each other, seemingly to avoid a black Chevy Suburban that had slewed across the road in front of them.

Within seconds, at the other end of the march on North Lakeshore Drive, as it crossed East Randolph, the lumbering Brinks armored trucks cut across all southbound lanes, blocking the road. Various SUVs uncovered .50 caliber Brownings fore and aft of the DHL and Brinks trucks. They spat tracers along the length of Randolph from both ends. Armor piercing rounds ricocheted off buildings. They smashed the reinforced glass in high rises. Lethal shards collapsed into the street. Marchers were caught between cascading debris and being ripped asunder by the machine gun bullets.

Both sets of trucks dumped false roofs. Their sides facing toward City Hall dropped down. This revealed 81mm mortars angled toward the march from both east and west. The first rounds were fed into the barrels and chugged upwards at high angles. Slowly but inexorably, they seemed to hang in the air above the buildings and marchers, most of whom were crawling along the roads and sidewalks through broken glass or running in panic down cross streets to avoid the gunfire.

At this point, two hotels to the north and two to the south that had been set with demolition charges blew up with a mighty roar and collapsed. There was nowhere left for the protestors to run. There were ten mortar barrels in all. Each was firing at a steady twenty rounds a minute. The deadly mortar-bombs were mixed. Some high explosive rounds were set to airburst lethal shrapnel from above. Others were fused to explode inside buildings, only after they had penetrated the roofs. White phosphorous bombs cascaded showers of glowing fragments. These also obscured the whole area in clouds of white smoke. Worse, these burned through protective clothing and seared through flesh to the bone.

Special Agent Calhoun, an FBI sniper in black body armor, was perched atop City Hall. At the sound of shooting and dull chugs from the mortars, he looked both east and west. Horrified he watched the mortar bombs flying high above and wobbling inexorably toward him. He radioed this in. Then he dove for the cover of the parapet as the first one exploded on the roof only feet away.

Two white phosphorous rounds blew up nearby. Calhoun choked on the smoke. He felt the incandescent chemicals. They melted much of his facemask, gloves and protective clothing.

White hot particles burned straight through his body to vital organs. Driven mad with pain, he rolled over the parapet without thinking. He plunged down onto a broken police line below, landing with a thud. Instant death was preferable to enduring the agony.

CHAPTER 15

Ending the Battle

The chaos caused by the attacks on the Chicago March left the FBI paralyzed. Individual agents were blinded by smoke, and beyond control. Those who could see, fired at men with weapons, glimpsed through the murk. Many fell, others fired back, spreading the mayhem. No one knew what was going on.

Much of Carver's view of the area below the John Hancock was obscured by rolling white smoke. He could see where the mortar shells were originating by their direction of arcs. He barked urgent orders.

"No firing in the downtown area! The attacks are coming from the perimeters! Get the boats closer to the shore! Scramble the choppers!"

Two of his helicopters, disguised as high-end civilian machines, surged upwards from the Midway airport on the lakeside. Two others swooped down from the west, where they had been circling a short distance from the city.

From the Willis Tower, a dismayed Special Agent Angelou also saw the origin of the attacking fire. The Deputy Director's arrogance had left her without response. The FBI's helicopters were way out at O'Hare airport on standby. They would be very late to intervene. Her agents in the city were reporting conflicts with armed men. *What the hell is happening?*

Her response was, "Fire on sight! Secure any shooters you can capture for questioning!"

She groaned, realizing her professional career was likely over.

<<>>

Bertha Newell, the alcoholic panhandler, whimpered. The loud bangs, gunfire and smoke terrified her. She crawled under her bench and pulled on a quart of cheap rum. She needed it now. The night may never come. Some people were running or staggering past her. They were shouting, screaming to each other,

"It's the BLA. They're killing us, destroying the city."

"Run for your lives."

A distraught woman yelled at Bertha.

"Where's my child? Her name's Bella. Have you seen her?"

Bertha couldn't understand what was happening. She shook her head. She moaned, took another pull on the bottle, and tried to wriggle face-down into the soft mulch of a flower bed behind the bench.

<<>>

Carver's two pristine white motor cruisers sped across the lake toward the shore in a great surge of power. They healed over into their turns leaving churning wakes. What had seemed mere playthings of the idle rich were transformed. On each a GAU-19/B, .50 cal Gatling gun was unmasked, ready, loaded. In seconds, they were spitting a, mixture of armor piercing and tracer rounds. These cut through the fake Brinks trucks and their defending SUVs like butter. The bodies of the BLA mortar crews were shredded and churned to bloody pulp. This stopped the bombardment from the east dead.

<<>>

Carver's two Midway based choppers flew just above the dense smoke as they crossed the city. They made their strafing runs from the north on the fake DHL trucks on Highway 51. They were followed by the two other aircraft from their holding patterns in the west. The Midway planes also mounted .50 cal Gatlings. The other two each loosed a salvo of four Brimstone air-to-surface missiles. These effectively blew a hole in the 51, engulfing all the surviving vehicles, and the hostile forces around them.

As the copters flew low from Midway, Angelou assumed they were terrorists. She screamed an order.

"Helicopter attack. Shoot them down!"

The pilot of the rear chopper was hit by an FBI sniper, firing from the roof of the Standard Oil building. The flyer slumped over his collective control. The aircraft slewed away, spiraling into the lake.

An over-zealous CNN helicopter, prompted by its Pulitzer Prize seeking reporter, strayed over the city center. It was buffeted by explosions and fires but was getting some unbelievable footage. A clearing in the smoke allowed another FBI sniper on the top of City Hall a deflection shot. He fired twice at the blurred image of the CNN chopper. Two rounds smashed through the glass cockpit. They cut through the turbines. The pilot struggled with the collective to control her turn. Without power, the machine fell into a stall. Its blades slashed into the side of Two Prudential Plaza, a nearby high-rise, and snapped off. The wreckage tumbled into the chaos below. It burst into a ball of flame. From a safe distance, other newshounds covered the deaths of their rivals with barely disguised relish.

Angelou closed her eyes in frustration. Then, she watched two other helicopters shooting up the BLA convoy on highway 51.

Who the hell are those guys?

<<>>

Dave, the deranged leader of the BLA, was holding a .45 pistol to the head of the pilot of another news copter. He and a buddy had commandeered it earlier, to give him the overview he wanted of the action. He saw the devastating counterattacks and the destruction of his men. Primeval fear took over.

"Get me the fuck out of here! Fly northwest! Hug the deck!"

CHAPTER 16

Aftershocks

The nation was in turmoil. Programs were interrupted. There was horrifying coverage from the news aircraft. This was interspersed with smoky and wobbly images from cell phones, mostly of falling debris or broken and bloody corpses. Incoherent screaming, explosions and collapsing buildings formed the soundtracks. Dust-choked, bleeding victims were running or staggering, some with cloths clamped over their mouths. It was like 9/11 all over again. Sirens wailed.

<<>>

Two hours later, the mayor of Chicago held a press conference on the steps of the Museum of Science and Industry near the lake, to the southeast of the devastated and still burning center. The cameras panned in from the background pillars of smoke to the north, to focus on the rostrum.

The mayor looked nervous, ducking and wincing slightly as emergency vehicle sirens blared along what was left of Lakeshore drive, to the north. There were still occasional gunshots.

A police helicopter circled overhead. AR-15 toting SWAT team members stood close around the mayor, suspicious eyes nervously moving left and right, scanning the press corps and others in the crowd. The media people seemed unusually chastened. Word of two lost news helicopters had spread.

There was an FBI agent standing prominently close behind the mayor. Special Agent Angelou was notably absent.

<<>>

The call reached her while she was still in the Willis Tower, swifter than she had expected. She gripped the scrambler phone tight. It was the Deputy Director, his voice dripping with malice.

“You’re suspended with immediate effect. You’re already facing disciplinary charges for negligence. You’ll be fully investigated. Your career’s over.”

With a curt, “Fuck you.” She replaced the phone, tossed her badge and gun onto a table, and stormed out of the office.

On the way down in the elevator, she ignored the FBI operative who was keeping the lift secure. Her heart was racing, her temples throbbing. *What can I do?*

As she walked through the lobby, her cell phone rang. She checked the screen. It was from someone called SecX. She remembered that as a math expression. Then she recalled it was also a subsidiary of a large private security firm. It was mostly employed by large corporations in difficult parts of the world and for U.S. government work in Iraq and Afghanistan. *What the hell! I'll take it.*

A laconic and rather gruff male voice spoke.

"Ex Special Agent Angelou. How's your day been? Mine's been rather good. Wanna talk?"

<<>>

During his next call, General Carver was reporting events to the Chairman of the Billionaires' Bonsai Club.

"We have had a major success, at the small cost of eleven casualties and three captured from our force. Our prisoners'll not talk. We'll try and break them out, but they know we'll care for their dependents if that fails. The civilian casualties you can on the TV would have happened anyway, collateral damage. We reckon there are thousands of dead.

"The important thing is we think we wiped out pretty much the whole BLA. We're following up on just one commandeered chopper that escaped and crash landed to the north.

"Yes sir, I know you want Bruce Kárpov. An we're gonna get the bastard. He must be feelin' pretty naked about now."

<<>>

The President went on national news from the White House. She looked especially angry and severe. She somberly read from her Autocue. Her face was suitably sad when expressing condolences for relatives and sympathy for the wounded. She looked sincere when she reinforced her support for the mayor of Chicago. Then her eyes flashed.

"Our nuclear forces have been put on DEFCON 3 until we can judge whether a hostile power is behind this heinous attack. The CIA is checking all sources.

"Let no one think that our great country will not retaliate. We have already suspended those whose negligence may have allowed this to happen.

"I've declared a federal state of emergency. The National Guard is on alert.

Significant investigatory and military resources are on their way to Chicago. FEMA will supply all the aid necessary to those left homeless or in need of help.

"I will not give up. I will not be satisfied; I will not rest until the perpetrators are dead or in jail."

Ten minutes later she was drinking a second martini in Marine One, on the way to a relaxing weekend at Camp David, thinking, *There's nothing like a good crisis to boost my presidential image.*

<<>>

On the morning news the day after the Chicago atrocities, there were various announcements. These included:

- Messages of sympathy and support from many countries.

- Denials of involvement by The Peoples' Republic of China, Russia and North Korea, in the face of various CIA, Mossad and British MI6 allegations and leaks that these countries may have been involved.

- The FBI offering rewards of $5 million each for information leading to the capture of Bruce Kárpov and Dave Golosz. They were now joint number ones on the most wanted list.

- The addition of Ex Special Agent Liza Angelou to the ten most wanted list. This was for, “Unlawful flight to avoid investigation into possible conspiracy, terrorism and murder charges.”

- Various retired generals, leaders of minor security firms, former FBI and CIA agents and a couple of psychiatrists were all building their bank balances and getting publicity on non-stop talking head shows.

<<>>

Schaumberg Illinois lies to the north of Chicago. In a basement beneath an office building, General Carver watched a monitor. It showed an interrogation in a secure room at an even lower level. Strapped to a steel chair, bolted to the concrete floor, a badly battered Dave Golosz bubbled bloody saliva from a smashed mouth and broken teeth. He’d been seized from a house in a Chicago suburb on a tip from an intercepted call to the FBI. The feds arrived too late to nab him. He was already in the trunk of a car heading for Schaumberg. When the FBI did arrive at the scene, they found the bullet riddled bodies of Golosz's three companions, survivors from the hotel bombers.

Sat opposite Dave Golosz in the basement and shocked by his appearance, Liza Angelou, the newest recruit to SecX, was interrogating him. His responses were groggy and slurred. His eyes glinted though badly bruised slits.

"Look I've told you, I've never met Bruce Kárpov. I've not even contacted him. I want a lawyer."

Carver hit a switch and his voice boomed around the cell.

"Enough of this! I'll be right in. Leave this to me, Liza."

She left the room as he entered. He was sucking on a cigar. In short order, two of his goons unshackled Dave, pulled down his pants and slammed him face down, spread across the steel table. Carver walked round so Dave could see him. He held a stick of dynamite with a short fuse in one hand. He lit it with his cigar. As it sputtered Dave screamed. Carver passed the explosive to a goon, who rammed it into Dave's rectum.

Dave stuck to his denial of knowing Bruce.

Carver and the goons left the room before the explosion. It shook the foundations and rattled the steel cell door against its frame.

<<>>

On a secure line, Carver spoke to the Bonsai Club chairman.

"The BLA is no more. The leader's dead. They were unrelated to Kárpov. Yes, I'm sure. He spilled the beans on a couple of others who may have escaped. They were amongst those who bombed the hotels. They'll be history within days, if they've survived so far. We'll net Kárpov next!

"Yes, Sir, don't worry. No one'll ever suspect us."

<<>>

The Guardian Newspaper, UK, The Washington Post, and CNN all received copies of the tapes, recorded from intercepts of FBI communications by SecX. They were a damning indictment of the Deputy Director. They revealed how he had stopped Angelou from dealing with the threat and how he had tried to pin the failure on her. Soon after the news broke, he was in custody.

Angelou was already using her skills and renewed contacts to track down Bruce. She was now a highly paid vice president of SecX. She wanted revenge on those Save the Bonsai bastards, and Carver had promised she would get it.

<<>>

In Tokyo, Aiko Okamoto, Daremo's twin, prepared to leave her house for lunch with her friends in the Ginza main shopping area. Maybe she would buy some expensive designer clothes. Her gilded life continued. She had married a rich banker and had a permanent live-in maid and chauffeur. The house was unusually large for Tokyo.

From a dark blue Honda Accord, farther up the street, an observer in dark glasses and wearing a hoodie watched Aiko's white-gloved chauffer drive his pampered passenger from the driveway in a black Mercedes-Maybach.

Leaving the Honda and pretending to be a jogger, the observer ran up past the now closed security gate. With surprising agility, the runner scaled the wall, dropping into the garden to approach the house. The intruder peeked in above the window sill and observed the maid vacuuming in a large room. The jogger entered the house through an unlocked back door.

<<>>

After the Chicago attacks, Bruce became even more paranoid. He knew the $5 million reward would motivate his betrayal by the leaders of the hippies in Sedona. He was aware that Sunshine still contacted them, even after he'd asked her not to. By the time the hippie cult leaders were calling the FBI to tell them where he and Sunshine were hiding out; the couple had already left for New Mexico.

Bruce was planning a border crossing to Ciudad Juarez when he became suspicious of the time Sunshine was spending in the motel bathroom. He put his ear to the door just in time.

"Look, just make sure I get the five mil. Yes. I'll keep him here till tomorrow."

When she re-entered the room he was gone, together with the false IDs passports and all their money.

"Fuck!"

She reached for her phone.

CHAPTER 17

Meeting of Minds?

Aiko Okamoto, Daremo's twin, returned from her shopping in the Ginza in the Maybach. To Aiko's annoyance her maid did not appear to help with the shopping. She had had to unlock the door herself. She would have words with her servant later. *Lazy old cow.*

Her chauffer held the house door open for her. Then he carried in the boxes and bags, stacking them in the hallway. Each item was exquisitely wrapped, as was normal in Japan. The chauffer went off to clean the car and put it in the garage. Aiko climbed the stairs to her bedroom. Something was wrong. The last remaining photograph she had of her parents, before their house burned down with them in it, lay on the bed. It should have been on the Shinto shrine downstairs. Her heart raced a little and she looked around the room. *Could the maid have put it there? Why would she do that?*

A stranger entered from her bathroom. There was something in the malevolent look in the shiny black eyes that stunned her into silence. Instinctively, she knew who it was. Daremo spoke.

“So, twin sister we meet at last.”

“You! What do you want? Get out or I’ll call for help.”

“No one’ll hear. Your maid is dead in that closet.”

Daremo would have liked to have prolonged the pleasure, but was worried about the whereabouts of the chauffer. S/he had to be satisfied with the terrified last look in Aiko’s eyes. S/he squeezed the life out of Aiko, jamming both thumbs deep into her windpipe till her eyes bulged and she stopped struggling. S/he tossed the body aside like a rag doll.

<<>>

Bruce's journey to Japan, took three months, used several aliases, and multiple disguises. His own mother would not have recognized him after plastic surgery in Valparaiso Chile. He even dressed in a burka to pass through Islamic Indonesia and Malaysia.

He arrived in the Japanese industrial port of Osaka on an ink-splattered, stinking squid boat. He hid in the fish hold during the routine customs check. The customs officers were normally sticklers for procedure, but in a hurry to move on to more salubrious vessels.

After dark, he lowered himself over the side and into Daremo's waiting black inflatable. S/he tried not to breathe in his disgusting smell. He was surprised when an androgynous, staccato voice spoke in stilted but precise English.

"Welcome to Osaka, Kárpov-san. I have been looking forward to meeting you for a long time."

Bruce was surprised when he saw Daremo. Part of him had built a fantasy of a sexy, but fascinating Japanese beauty, who would give him the usual adulation. What he saw puzzled him. Inside the lumpy lifejacket s/he could be man or woman. S/he wore a blue baseball cap with a large letter D on the front. The hat hid any hair. He assumed the D was for Daremo. Later, s/he explained the cap represented the Nagoya baseball team, the Chinichi Dragons.

He was just desperate to get a hot bath, a rest, and freedom from pursuit.

Daremo had intended to drive all the way to the laboratory without stopping, but decided to check into a motel to get him cleaned up. He really reeked. S/he drove with the window down and with face turned away as much as possible, to avoid his stench. Hopefully, his large bag contained a change of clothing.

<<>>

The next morning, with him feeling cleaner, Bruce and Daremo resumed their journey. There was still a lingering stench, but it was bearable.

S/he told him about some of the work at the laboratory. He only half listened. It all sounded like a scientific fantasy. All he cared about now was reaching a place of sanctuary and ending his months long escape run. Through tired eyes, he watched the green countryside and villages rolling by for what seemed hours. He dozed off in the comfortable seat of the Lexus SUV.

<<>>

He woke shortly before Daremo turned off onto a dirt track.

“We are nearly there, Kárpov-san. Just a few more kilometers.”

He saw that the cap was gone and was surprised to see a perfectly shaven head. *Is it a man or woman? Anyway, what a disappointment! Sex with this one is out of the question.*

<<>>

Daremo leaned out of the window for a laser scanner at the gate. S/he presented the right iris to be read. A heavy portal swung open and a massive metal barrier swiveled down into the ground. Bruce noticed huge tropical plants either side of a gravel driveway. *I could swear they're shivering and swaying as we pass. It's creepy.*

A large, low-rise building was partially built into a hill. It would be difficult to spot from above. Another laser scanner allowed Daremo and Bruce passage through a steel entrance door. He was amazed to see no people. Various robots, intent on unknown missions, whirred eerily past on rubber wheels.

<<>>

His room was spartan but adequate. Daremo had provided a TV with satellite access to various English language stations. There was a small desk, a top of the line Apple computer and a chair. Ignoring all else, he crashed out on the Japanese style futon, a sort of puffy thin mattress. It was spread on a woven rush mat, but was surprisingly comfortable. He slept for 18 hours.

<<>>

Next day's tour of the facility took three hours. Every minute was packed with wonder and foreboding. He could hardly take it all in.

The clean-rooms housing the cloning and gene modification technology were beyond his comprehension. Daremo's explanations flew right over his head. He was impressed and horrified to see the huge carnivorous plants. They seemed to be whispering to each other and bending in his direction. Robots were feeding squealing, live rodents to them with their mechanical arms. They too were scary.

"For your own safety, stay close to me Kárpov-san. The plants will need to learn that you are a friend and with me. The robots are programmed not to harm humans unless attacked."

He felt especially nervous when they passed close to various menacing and swaying plants. He stuck to Daremo like glue. S/he rattled off each hybrid species and its characteristics. Proudly, Daremo told him that s/he could modify most hybrids to thrive in any climate zone.

The stink in some areas was stomach churning. S/he explained that some of the carnivorous plants lured their prey with the smell of rotting flesh. He was very uncomfortable, sweating slightly. *But I've no place else to run. Best keep Daremo sweet.*

<<>>

That evening, they sat down to eat at a table with a gas burner in its center.

"Kárpov-san I am going to prepare shabu-shabu, a hotpot dish."

He watched as s/he set a cookpot on the burner and added a cabbage-like vegetable, spring onions and mushrooms. While it stewed, they drank sake.

Before him was a plate of very thinly sliced, well-marbled beef. Daremo showed him how to dip a piece of meat into the hotpot with his chopsticks. When it turned a light color, it was ready. Then he was to dip it into the sesame sauce and eat it right away. *Mm, a little different, but not bad. Better than all that damned raw fish and seaweed on the squid boat.*

He washed the meal down with more warm sake. Daremo introduced local customs.

"In Japan it is considered impolite to pour oneself a drink. Your companion keeps your cup full and you theirs."

"Sounds like we'll become best friends then."

"I hope so Bruce-san. That is important, but more important is you helping to spread my lovely plants around the world.

"I experimented by hiring three private cargo planes with disreputable pilots. One just dumped seeds from high altitude. The others were supposed to drop small trees and self-planting seedlings. One plane crashed in the Brazilian jungle. Another flew into a mountain in the Urals. It was all too risky for me. These types of people are dangerous and may have military or CIA links."

From what he'd seen and heard so far, Bruce was doubtful that getting involved was a great idea. *Best keep quiet about that for now.*

As the evening wore on, Daremo became a little drunk and loosened up. S/he explained the unique genetic condition that s/he had and a bit about the past. He seemed shocked and said it was sad that anyone could be treated so.

S/he felt he was listening and sympathetic. *I'm sure we can make a great partnership. I hadn't realized how un-Japanese he is. I hope he can adapt. I'll try to make him feel at home.*

CHAPTER 18

Get Bruce Kárpov

The town of Sahuarita, Arizona, lies about 15 miles south of Tucson. Its environs played a vital part in the USA's cold war programs. Apart from an enormous airstrip, the area provided bombing ranges. In particular, there were silos for launching Intercontinental Ballistic Missiles. Before the SALT treaties, these weapons were an essential part of the USA's nuclear deterrent.

<<>>

Senior Vice President Liza Angelou looked down on the desert and small township from her SecX Bombardier Global 8000 jet, as it made a gentle turn to line up on the concrete runway. The surrounding desert was rugged and unappealing. Nonetheless, this was to be her home base. It was where General Carver had established his secret global operations center.

The plane's extra tanks gave it a 10,000-mile range, making it suitable for intercontinental travel without refueling. It and its sister aircraft were the only ones fitted with military air-to-air refueling capability to add further range if needed. They required USAF cooperation to accomplish this. Extensive government contracts assured that this would be forthcoming. The military saw SecX as an extension of its own reach for black programs and sensitive operations, usually of an illegal nature.

The plane's normal configuration was for up to 18 seats, but this one had only seven ultra-luxurious berths. Its communications and electronics equipment more than doubled the normal $75 million cost. The engines were upgraded to provide additional power to compensate for the extra weight and for operations in hot climates. These two aircraft served as Carver's equivalents of Air Force One. Angelou smiled at the thought that one was available to her if she needed to set off in hot pursuit of Bruce Kárpov. *We have to find the bastard first. But I will get him!*

They landed with the usual bump and squeal of tires. Then the engines reversed thrust to reduce their speed. The plane taxied into a bomb-proof hangar without pause. This building was mostly hidden beneath the desert floor at the far side of the airfield. Only the ramp down and steel doors could be seen, and then only from up close.

Inside the hangar, from the plane's steps, she noted several other aircraft. They included a couple of old A10 Thunderbolt tank busters in good condition and four Black Hawk choppers. The place was crawling with armed guards in military style uniforms.

Without any fanfare, a grim-faced jar-head blurted out, "Welcome to Sahuarita, Ma'am." Avoiding further conversation, he dumped her suitcase in the back of a desert camouflaged Humvee. He and his driver jumped into the front seats. She clambered in behind them. They roared up another ramp at the rear of the hangar toward the surface, exiting via a back-entranceway. A plume of dust from the dirt roads followed the speeding vehicle.

A mile away, they showed IDs to vigilant guards before entering an enormous razor-wired compound that seemed to stretch as far as the eye could see. A few hundred yards farther and a massive blast-proof door rumbled slowly open. It closed behind them, to again swallow them into the depths of the earth.

<<>>

Bruce could see that his host was a bio-engineering genius. He learned that hacking was another of Daremo's skills, but he prided himself on being superior. He hadn't realized how limited was the professor's knowledge of both the world of commerce and of life outside of Japan. *Well, I must seem as ignorant of things Japanese as Daremo is of my world. I'm very dependent on Daremo. I'm probably expendable too. Better figure out how to make myself useful. I wouldn't like to get on Daremo's bad side. Things get slashed to pieces with those traditional weapons she keeps around here. That's scary.*

Bruce took to wearing the long Japanese robe known as a yukata. He selected one with a blue crane design and flowing sleeves. It kept him cool in the dry summer heat. He learned to keep the sleeves from dragging in his food.

"Ah, good choice Bruce-san. Cranes are a sign of fidelity. We are bound together with trust now."

"May I respectfully make a suggestion, professor? I think I have some ideas as to how to spread some of your plants around the world. Relying on the natural way will take a thousand years"

He has discovered politeness. Maybe he is learning our ways.

<<>>

It took Senior Vice President Angelou over a week to begin to feel comfortable in her new quarters. The furnishings were fine, if somewhat masculine. The deadening silence of the yards-thick reinforced-concrete roof and grey-painted, windowless walls hardly made it a home.

As expense seemed no object, she decided to add some extravagant female touches. She had window-size plasma monitors added to all the rooms. They were programmable to screen any topography she fancied worldwide, along with suitable background noises. These replaced the dominant electronic hum of the massive modified Minuteman 1 silo.

During breakfast, she could look down over Central Park, New York. At a touch of a control or voice command, she was viewing the island coastline of Bora Bora in the Pacific. This was accompanied by tropical birdsong, the gentle lapping of the waves. Balmy breezes ruffled the coconut palms.

She could have any painting she liked and change it at will. She preferred female and feminist artists like Frida Kahlo, Georgia O'Keefe and Anita Steckel.

Angelou thought the SecX facility was awesome. *It must have cost hundreds of millions, maybe even billions, to convert and equip. The main War Room houses at least 10,000 square feet of electronics. It's suspended from the hardened roof on enormous cushioning springs. It can take a direct hit and survive. Carver boasted that it was designed to withstand a strike from a ten-megaton missile... Let's hope we don't have to find out if that's true.*

Data was relayed here from the corporation's worldwide information centers and from phone-taps and hacks into the networks of U.S. and foreign clandestine services around the globe.

The latest supercomputers were served by hundreds of techies and analysts working in shifts. They presented their reports on the cinema-sized screen to the leadership team. Carver and his senior staff could also access any of these from his other locations, as well as from his aircraft.

<<>>

At Bruce's request, Daremo provided him a plant-free area for exercise and to chill out, just outside the main laboratory buildings. Thoughtfully, s/he had added a couple of white-painted Adirondack chairs, a gas barbecue and a fridge full of Sam Adams beer, his favorite.

He worked away designing a seed spreading campaign. It was based on those used to distribute drugs ordered via the dark web. The target customers were gardening fanatics and conservationists in every country. Bruce persuaded Daremo that the more fearsome carnivorous plants should be excluded, at least in the short term.

"This'll ensure repeat orders. If the plants start eating the growers, it'll stop 'em buying more and reduce our customer base."

"As you wish Bruce-san."

He does not realize that some of my green friends can release deadly gases. Maybe I should keep some things from him. He seems a little sensitive.

<<>>

One sunny afternoon, in a Sam Adams induced stupor Bruce dozed off in one of his chairs. A dark green, leafy tendril reached stealthily through the wire fence some yards away. It seemed to thicken and strengthen as it crept slowly along the raked gravel of his compound. It spiraled up and around the arm of his chair.

He yelled and screamed in pain. The thing had grabbed his arm in a vice-like grip. A vicious little orifice opened at the tip. It sliced off the end of a finger in one bite. Blood poured out. It seemed about to take a bigger bite. He bellowed in anguish. Other fronds were slithering menacingly toward him.

Hearing his shouts, Daremo leapt over the fence carrying a wooden najinata. Gently, so as not to harm the plants, s/he prized his arm free with the spear's blunted tip and pushed aside the other tendrils with the haft. They withdrew when they sensed the familiar presence.

S/he bowed deeply to Bruce as he whimpered. "So sorry Bruce-san. I made a terrible mistake. I promise to find a way to make it up to you."

S/he expertly bound up his finger with a dressing. He bit back an angry remark. His eyes watered with the added sting from the antiseptic. He just gave Daremo a hard stare, biting on his tongue to hold back a retort. *And just how can you compensate for the loss of a finger-end you frigging weirdo. What happens, if they attack again?*

<<>>

Angelou and Carver received their first solid lead for some weeks. An FBI asset had ordered samples of seeds on the dark web. On receipt he sent them to a federal bio-science and genetics lab. SecX intercepted the results before the FBI received them. The lab was cultivating some of the seeds, but had also identified pollens clinging to one of them. These were from species of bamboo and other plants that could only have come from the largest Japanese Island, Honshu. Angelou was exultant.

"At last, we now have a country to focus on."

They decided to develop plans whilst on their way to investigate in person. Their plane powered high over the Pacific.

Angelou knew from experience that the FBI would still be mired in evaluating the data. After that, it would take them time to negotiate how to deal with the Japanese. This would start with getting the State Department to agree on an approach. After that there would be negotiations with the Japanese government. All this could take weeks. Meanwhile, SecX was already readying a rapid reaction team, free from such diplomatic and legal niceties.

SecX's Tokyo station head and three of his people were driving to meet Carver and Angelou at Narita airport. Suites at the Imperial Hotel were being prepared for them and swept for electronic spying devices.

Eventually, the SecX plane landed at Narita. It taxied into a private hangar. The three Japanese bowed deeply as Carver and Angelou stepped down from the aircraft.

<<>>

Daremo kept a discreet check on Bruce's internet connections. This was partly to learn from his superior hacking skills. Additionally, it ensured that the professor was fully informed as to the successful distribution of seeds to plant activists all over the world. Lastly, it satisfied an almost paranoid concern about tight security.

With satisfaction, s/he noted that he routed all of his traffic via encrypted hacks through servers in Russia, China and North Korea. S/he was amused to see from the media that the FBI and the U.S. government were still blaming these nations for the deaths of over 8,000 people in the Chicago massacre.

Daremo also noted Bruce's regular access to internet porn sites. He seemed to like those where the male had two women at the same time. *Why do so many men like this idea? They have only one penis. I really don't understand.*

Sex had never interested Daremo in any physical or emotional way, but s/he had researched the mechanics. *It is puzzling that sex drives otherwise clever people to wildly irrational and bizarre behavior.* S/he decided on a way to restore Bruce to happiness.

<<>>

Daremo's robots bustled around the clock. They nurtured and propagated plants. They collected and packaged the seeds. They dispatched them abroad, disguised as other products and by various routes. They were then posted or couriered from different locations around the world. The U.S. Postal Service, Deutsche Post, FedEx, and hundreds of other couriers became unwitting transporters of doom. Amazon and its many much smaller rivals won a large part of the distribution business.

Unbeknown to Bruce, Daremo's favorite carnivorous and toxic plant varieties were now included in many of the packages.

<<>>

In the valley of the Tualatin River, southwest of Portland Oregon, The Mitchell family grew their organic vegetables. They also kept a few free-range hens, baked cakes, and grew skunk cannabis. They had a regular stall at the Beaverton Farmers market. It was the biggest in the area. Life was good. Their kids were homeschooled. They felt they lived a healthy and safe life. They became passionate growers of threatened and exotic species of plants.

<<>>

The mother, thirty-eight-year old Jackie Mitchell, was the one who encountered the ad through social media:

Help Save the Planet

We have developed plants that can survive global warming. They can even help reverse it. Let us know your climate zone. We will guarantee success.

These plants, trees and shrubs are beautiful and environmentally friendly.
They can also provide you with a good income as you help save the environment.
You achieve this by selling them on to other enthusiasts.

Who could resist? Fake endorsements and testimonials were provided.

The Mitchells were already dealing their skunk through the dark web, so it all worked very smoothly. Their deliveries of the amazing plants came from the Netherlands, via a well-known home delivery firm.

The first specimens grew amazingly rapidly. They looked healthy and seemed immune to insect attacks. They were ready for market in just a few weeks. Some developed interesting flowers and fruits.

The family transplanted them into bio-degradable fiber pots and loaded them into their old Chevy pickup, along with their honey, some home-made cakes, and brownies. These cookies were laced with sufficient skunk to give a buzz with every bite. They were a best seller.

CHAPTER 19

Unfortunate Incidents

Bruce had been chilling in the sun with a few beers. Since losing his finger end, he always kept a wary eye on his boundary fence. Frequent nightmares of slithering tendrils eating him alive disturbed his sleep.

To get out of the heat, he opened the door to his quarters in the main building, expecting to sit and work at his computer. To his surprise, two very attractive Japanese girls were in the room. The one sitting in his chair had dyed blond hair. She wore an ultra mini tartan school uniform with white bobby socks. The other was dressed totally in pink and sprawled seductively on his futon. Fluffy pink cat's ears were part of her costume. She sported a spectacular boob job and cleavage. She winked and threw him a salacious smile. The pink cat-girl spoke.

"Welcome home Bruce-san, Professor Daremo asked us to comfort you. My name is Sekushina Onnanoko. My friend is Babi Ningyo. You can call us Babi and Seku."

Bruce felt a little strange being confronted by two Japanese girls who seemed only to want to do his bidding. It wasn't that he hadn't enjoyed getting laid by groupies when he became notorious. He'd had dozens of steamy sessions with Sunshine too. But there was something disconcerting about how the Japanese liked their women. He'd seen the schoolgirl outfits in Japanese porno movies. He knew it wasn't pedophilia, as the sex workers involved were all of age.

Despite this, and emboldened by his beer drinking outside, he thought, *Why not? The girls have a sexy musky smell. There's something different about the way their skin feels. It must be a Japanese trait. Still, their flesh is firm and warm with a silky softness. Their dark underarm and pubic hair feels great and they're wet with desire.*

As he thrust into Seku, she gave little rhythmic moans. The Japanese women in his movies did this too. He always thought it sounded as though they were in pain.

Seku rolled on top of him and started a wild ride. He gasped as her inner muscles squeezed his member and started to milk it. He climaxed and pulled her down on top of him. Her inner muscles were gripping too tightly. He needed her to stop, fearing she might wrench off his receding erection. As she came nearer his ear there was a sound. *What's that whirring I hear?*

He threw her off, his suspicions aroused.

"Babi, come here."

He sat on his chair bending the naked girl over his knee. He carefully examined every inch of her. Her pubic hair was definitely human. Under a blond wig, he found the access panel to an electronic board full of chips and devices.

"My god! You're both robots! What a turn off!"

What am I doing? This is nuts. It's horrible.

Seku smiled at him, pushing together her ample breasts with their realistic brown nipples.

"Yes Bruce-san. We are robots, programmed to be whatever is your pleasure. We do whatever you want. You can teach us."

He raised his eyes to the ceiling.

<<>>

It was the day before Bruce's escapade with the robots. In Oregon, Jackie Mitchell focused on keeping her family healthy, safe and unpolluted by the world outside the farm, as usual.

This day, she helped load the pickup. Then she ensured the kids were securely seated and belted into the vehicle. Some of the farm-roads were bumpy and unpaved. The drive to the market took about an hour.

At the market, Mom and Pop Mitchell set out their wares. The older kids ran around renewing friendships. Only four-year-old Dylan hung about the plants in the stall. He picked up a small leafy plant with attractive orange pods among the leaves. He took it to his favorite hiding place beneath the table. A green tarp below the plants hid him from view.

His parents were doing a roaring trade, smiling at their customers, giving growing tips and collecting the money. Little Dylan was far from their minds.

Dylan poked a tiny finger into the nicely sticky black earth around his plant's roots and smiled. One of the pods on his new toy plaything seemed just asking to be squeezed. He crushed it between his thumb and forefinger. A puff of vapor escaped and went straight into his eyes and mouth. He tried to stand but fell forward from under the tarp. He foamed at the mouth, making croaking noises. His lips turned blue. He was dead before he hit the ground.

An old lady saw him fall, put her hands to her face in horror and screamed. His mother ran to help him. Several other pods burst, responding to the message that the plant was under attack. They wafted a toxic dust from under the table. The slight breeze dispersed it around the area.

Jackie Mitchell's corpse slumped across the body of her son. Several others ran to the scene. They too started to foam and collapse. Those not yet affected fled. Some stumbled no farther than a few yards. Other plants on the stall, and some already being borne away by customers in pickups reacted. A driver collapsed over the wheel of his truck. The vehicle veered into a tree. Its horn blared till the battery ran down.

<<>>

SecX's task force was assembling in the outskirts of Atsugi, a small town to the southeast of Tokyo. Five containers of specialized equipment and arms were delivered via the port of Yokohama. The warehouse was full of men checking and loading weapons and preparing for action.

SecX's intelligence specialists were evaluating every known bio-lab and growing area in Japan. They monitored internet traffic; reviewed data from U.S. military satellites and fed it all into super computers at their operations center in the Minuteman silo. The algorithms identified anomalies and patterns.

In Atsugi, General Carver's red phone rang. He motioned for Angelou to listen in. Nothing came in on that phone unless it was A1 priority.

"We think we've found something sir. Look at your monitor.

"The area circled in blue is supposed to be undeveloped farm land. We see dense foliage growing in an organized way. Now watch as we switch to the images from a Chinese satellite's thermal cameras. It flew over less than an hour ago. It shows a lot of power use and a significant underground facility. It's hidden from normal overhead surveillance. The authorities here have no records of any known businesses or bio-labs and research fields in that area. There seem to be large amounts of encrypted signals coming from the location too. This could be it."

General Carver dispatched a reconnaissance team, equipped with drones and all they needed to evaluate the potential target. An attack force was preparing to leave once the target was confirmed.

"Looks like we might have him, Angelou. Get ready to move out."

<<>>

SecX's recce-team leader was hidden in the undergrowth within sight of the target area. He reported to Carver on a scrambler phone. Carver and Angelou were already speeding toward the lab in the lead ship of 20 Black Hawk helicopters carrying the strike force.

"Yes, General, it's definitely the place. Our drone got positive ID on the target; Bruce Kárpov just came out through a side door from the underground lab. I'm sending the picture now."

Carver and Angelou were delighted. There was their quarry, laid back in an Adirondack chair, drinking a beer. Angelou was excited.

"We've got him at last, chief! Will it be dead or alive?"

Carver rolled his cigar into the corner of his mouth.

"It will definitely be dead, but not before he's told us exactly what the hell's been going on. We've been getting reports of deaths from strange plants coming in from around the world. At least 30 incidents. Everyone's panicking. If I hadn't shared what we know with the State Department, there'd be a nuclear war by now."

<<>>

Daremo was checking on the animal feed stocks when a red light started flashing in the ceiling. S/he rushed back to the control room. The plants outside were going frantic and had set off the motion detectors. S/he pulled up some remote cameras around the property. One of them picked up a two-man team hiding in some scrub. They were in military uniforms. They had a spotting scope focused on the main security gate. *Damn! We need to move fast.*

S/he pushed a few controls to activate the defenses, strapped on two swords and rushed to Bruce's quarters. S/he pushed his bell. When the door opened, s/he was surprised to see the two robots, switched off and sitting naked in a corner. *Hmm. There's no time to worry about that now.*

"Come on! We have to get out of here, we're about to be attacked."

Daremo's obvious urgency sent Bruce into action mode. His old fears kicked in. He grabbed his ever-ready emergency backpack. Then, he followed Daremo through a secret door s/he opened in a metal wall. Behind it was a passage and stairs leading downwards. He felt the concrete treads shaking from heavily muffled explosions coming from somewhere behind them.

A short distance farther and Daremo motioned him to squeeze into a cramped streamlined capsule. S/he settled into the back seat and closed the door to the tube that contained it. He was impressed. *Wow a hyperloop. S/he must have had this installed with some of the millions I sent via Frankfurt. How did s/he get it done in secret? Shouldn't ask. There are bound to be engineers' bodies somewhere.*

A powerful jet of air whisked the vehicle off on a 400 kilometer per hour journey down the dead straight tube. It was similar to the way that 1930s department stores sent money from cashiers around the store. They put the cash in small capsules, and then propelled them through pneumatic tubes to the cash center in the basement. The vehicle seemed to slow almost instantly, as it arrived at its terminus, kilometers away.

<<>>

SecX's Black Hawks unloaded the attack force into and around the compound surrounding the lab. Carver and Angelou's command chopper circled above to give them eyes-on control. Their video feeds showed explosions in multiple places. From the Black Hawk's windows they could see flashes of light and smoke emerging through the vegetation. On the monitors, they saw close-ups of one of the recon teams being blown to pieces. Smoke soon blanketed the area. Carver switched to infrared vision, listening to the confusion amongst his forces.

“We’re fixing the shaped charges to the main lab entrance now.”

There was a loud bang.

“Okay, we’re in.”

Another bang followed. Then more.

“The place’s mined. Men down. MediVac! MediVac!”

There were screams. A report from another team outside the buildings was accompanied by video from their helmet cameras.

“OK, were walking through some nasty looking plants. Jesus!”

Carver saw a huge Venus flytrap snap shut on one of the men who stumbled over its trigger-hairs. Another trooper was entangled in the spines of a rattan plant. It seemed to be wrapping about his body armor like a huge snake, probing for weak spots. It found them. The man roared with pain. Other troops were firing into the plants. They seemed to just absorb the bullets. Carver yelled.

“Keep going, we have to get the bastard!”

<<>>

Two hours and many casualties later, desultory reports were coming from inside.

“This place is weird. We’ve found a roomful of caged rats. There are robots working here.”

Carver responded.

“Grab some of ’em. We need the intel.”

“Yes, Sir.”

There were multiple blasts as the bots exploded when touched. A trooper reported from another area.

“I think I’ve found Kárpov’s room. There’re two Jap girls here. Are they dead? Wow! They’re dummies! There’s a computer.”

Desperately, Angelou shouted.

“Don’t touch it! Wait for the munitions disposal team.”

There was an earthshaking, Whump! The trooper was blown into the air. From the chopper, they saw a huge fireball erupting through the roof of the underground lab. Black smoke billowed upwards.

Another man shouted from somewhere.

“I’ve found what might be an escape tunnel. It’s been blocked with explosives.”

Angelou threw Carver a despairing look.

“He’s gotten away. He can’t have gone far.”

Carver looked grim, chomping on his cigar.

“All forces withdraw. Regroup. Then search the surrounding area.

“The Japanese Self-Defense Force choppers are five minutes out. They can join in with the search. Now, move!”

CHAPTER 19

On the Brink

A week later, back in their U.S. Minuteman bunker, Angelou and Carver were sifting through incoming intel. Most of SecX's people had been expelled from Japan following the debacle. Fortunately, some of those secretly embedded in the Japanese Self-Defense Forces and administration were still operational.

The plant attacks in major cities around the world eclipsed recent incidents in Japan. They were watching Fox News on a big screen. Scenes of rioting and looting were showing from most major U.S. cities. The death toll from plant attacks was already in the hundreds of thousands in the U.S. alone. The rest of the world suffered the same or worse, but Fox was giving that less coverage.

The President appeared in a live broadcast. She looked tired but did her best to appear in control.

“We are facing a greater threat to our nation and the world than has ever occurred in human history. Our legislature has given my administration emergency powers. That is why there are curfews and martial law.

“Looters, and those trying to disrupt our response, will be shot on sight. I say this with regret, but the future of the entire human race is at stake. We must all be resolute and make sacrifices. Our great nation must and will survive. We will lead the world out of this catastrophe.

“I’m sorry. We cannot take questions. I have to return to the War Room to manage our response.”

Carver could see that SecX was being sidelined. Many of his people had gone AWOL. He addressed Angelou.

“Let’s take stock. First, what seems to work in killing these plants?”

Angelou rattled off the salient points from the reports coming in.

“Napalm is only effective locally. The U.S. is using defoliants, as it did in Vietnam. The issues there are that the stocks held were illegal and clandestine. They’re nearly all used up. We know that there’ll be years of cancer and crop devastation as a result.”

He growled at her.

“The hell with that. We face an existential threat. What else can be done?”

“The problem is that manufacturing more chemicals on the scale needed would require major logistics and raw materials. The Air Force and Army are supplying the transport but it’ll take months to get significant production on line. Demonstrators are trying to stop this. Food supplies will be disrupted and polluted for years to come.”

He finally lost his temper, spluttering and banging his fist on the table. She jerked back in surprise. He roared.

"What a clusterfuck! We shoot the demonstrators and seize control of supplies. What else can be done?"

Struggling to keep calm, she looked at him coldly. *Maybe I joined the wrong team. What does money matter now?*

"General, you need to realize that SecX is sidelined. There is little we can do. The forces we have around here in the desert are pretty much all we can rely on now. The government's shutting us out. The only reason we know what's going on is that we still have people in the major intelligence agencies."

Furious, Carver screamed at her.

"Crap! Information is power. What is the government planning? They can't cut us out."

Angelou kept her cool.

"The primary issue is that only nuclear forces can be deployed immediately. The U.S. administration is looking into the effects of radiation on plants. It's crazy. They'd have to use the nukes on U.S. territory, and the immediate and lasting effects on the population don't bear thinking about.

"I've taken a quick look at the predicted effectiveness of nukes. Obviously, the explosion incinerates everything within the immediate radius of the blast. The soil in that area is devoid of nutrients as they are all torched. Further out, different plant species show varying damage from X-ray, gamma, and other radiation. Not enough is known to be certain how these particular plants will react. I don't think nukes can work. Remember the vegetation around the nuclear meltdown in

Chernobyl in the Ukraine. Plants are still thriving, even though the radiation killed humans. I also hope that no one would be crazy enough to try nukes."

General Carver gave her a wicked smile, puffing out his chest.

"At times like these, what you think is irrelevant. This is what I'm about. Leaders need to take decisive action. People will die. That's just how it is.

"Angelou, you're relieved of duty. I want you to go to your quarters. You will stay there. All your passwords and access will be withdrawn. Now, get out! I've got to figure how to get control of U.S. nuclear forces. The president's just a goddamned woman. She has to be superseded."

Utterly shocked, Angelou stalked out of the room. She went to her room and verified the magazine on her Glock was full. She clicked it back into place. *Somehow, he must be stopped.*

<<>>

Daremo despised Bruce's weakness. As s/he pushed on through some paddy fields in the dark, he was stumbling, moaning, and lagging behind. S/he was already carrying both of their escape packs.

"Come on Bruce-san. If we don't get to the next village before daylight, we'll be caught."

"I can't go on Daremo. I'm exhausted. Maybe we should give ourselves up. How bad could it be? I'm cramping up. Just a little rest, please."

S/he was dragging him along by one arm now. Zen focus tuned out Daremo's own tiredness. *I'll start over when we get away from here. The work must continue. Do I really need him? He's a great disappointment. Still he may yet be of use.*

Daremo pushed, pulled, and persuaded Bruce to keep going long after his body gave up. Eventually, well after dawn, s/he dumped him by the roadside. After a half-hour devoid of traffic, s/he waved down a passing motorist. He opened the passenger door to offer a lift. Daremo seized him by one hand, twisting it into an excruciating Aikido-hold. She yanked him from the car, driving an elbow through the side of his skull. S/he dumped his body in a ditch. Bruce was beyond caring and fell asleep in the back seat, as s/he drove away.

An hour later a flight of Mitsubishi F2Bs roared low overhead. They sported the blood red disc of the Japanese Air Self-Defense Force. The fighter bombers climbed and circled once. Far behind the car, the leader winged over and dived. Five fat napalm tanks tumbled from under the wings and fuselage, laying a streak of explosive fire over some trees. The others followed in line, carpeting the area where the fields of plants lived. Daremo glowered at the bursting orange flames in the rearview mirror.

“Murderers! We have to fight back.”

Awakened by the screaming jet engines, Bruce could only moan.

CHAPTER 20

Escaping the Pain

Musing in her federal prison cell, Bruce Kárpov's ex-girlfriend, Sunshine, felt hard-done by. *I shared all I knew with the FBI. They should've given me some of the five-million reward. It wasn't my fault they let Brucie escape. Now, I'm stuck in this top security prison, awaiting trial without bail. They say I'm a terrorist. That's crazy; I'm just a hippie free spirit. I don't even understand some of the charges. What the fuck is wire fraud?*

Her interrogators tried to use her to entice Bruce Kárpov into the open. All her media posts and other attempts went unanswered. Her "Brucie" had clearly moved on. She had nothing to sell to the feds, so they tossed her to the wolves. It made them look better.

In the jail, there were ways she could get a heroin fix from the trustees. They delivered books and her food. A recycled syringe and a small packet of badly cut heroin could be slipped through in a hollowed book. The library trustee lusted after Sunshine's lithesome body. Sunshine's cigarettes were a bonus. The trustee's fantasies focused on the day Sunshine would join the other inmates, after her trial. For now, she frenziedly stretched her arm through the door flap to grope Sunshine. It was part-payment for her deliveries.

Sunshine was at that stage of desperation where she would do anything for a fix. The rush of euphoria, the white light and the oblivion were a relief from the utter boredom of isolation.

Her heroin trustee missed a few shifts. As a result, Sunshine was soaking with sweat. She couldn't think straight due to the delirium and fever of withdrawal. She was desperate for a fix. Her nose was running. She vomited back her food. Her aching joints lanced pain every time she moved. The cramps in her bowels and diarrhea added to her misery. The craving never stopped. The depression and despair became overwhelming.

<<>>

In a small room deep under the White House, the president was taking a quick nap. After 20 hours without sleep, she needed it. An aid knocked on the door, dragging her reluctantly back to consciousness. Bleary eyed, she opened and read the decrypted message.

For Your Eyes Only - Extremely Urgent

This is from ex-FBI Special Agent Angelou. I oversaw the FBI's response to the Chicago attack. I am imprisoned in SecX's operational HQ. It is in refurbished Minuteman silo No. 22.

General Carver, Chairman and Chief Executive Officer of SecX has embedded agents in all your security forces and the White House staff. He plans to seize control of all U.S. nuclear forces and unleash them to try and destroy the

> *plants. He is deranged and must be stopped.*

Now fully alert, the president looked at her aid.

"Is that all?"

"Yes, Madam President."

"Jesus H. Christ! How do we know if it's genuine?"

She thought in silence for a moment.

"Get Admiral Weaver in here right away. Be discrete, No one should see that his coming here is important.

"As soon as he's left, I want to meet with the Joint Chiefs of Staff. We can't risk our military thinking there's an attack on the U.S. and starting World War III.

"Immediately after that, I need to speak to the Russian and Chinese presidents on the hot lines. They need to know what's happening."

<<>>

Carver was shocked when one of his cryptographers, tapped him on the arm.

"Sir, an unauthorized coded message has been sent from inside our building."

"What?

"How?

"What's it say?"

"Don't know, Sir. We're working on it."

He yelled for his head of security.

"Bring me Angelou. It must be her. She must have set something up anticipating this."

<<>>

Angelou had smashed the access control to her steel door. SecX security guards had to blow it off its hinges. Through the smoke and dust, she shot the first three men through the door in their heads with her Glock .45. Others, wearing body armor, piled into the room, and overwhelmed her. They dragged her, kicking, and struggling, to face Carver.

He slapped her hard across the face. Her head rocked back. She spat a tooth dislodged by his West Point class ring.

"You Fucking Bitch! What was in the transmission?"

"What transmission?"

He set to work on her systematically, with his fists and burning cigar.

Through bloody lips and spitting blood, she croaked, “Didn’t they teach you that torture doesn’t work”

He grunted with the effort of breaking a cheek bone with a punch.

“Sure did, but I enjoy it.”

<<>>

The captain of the newly commissioned Columbia Class SSBN submarine, the USS Franklin D. Roosevelt, was in his cabin writing his log. The boat was on its shakedown cruise. It was at a depth of 500 feet off the Atlantic coast of the USA, in full stealth mode. She carried 16 Trident II D5 missiles. Each had multiple, independently targeted, warheads. They began their trajectory carried in a “bus.” This was like a seed pod of nukes and decoys. Dispersed high above the atmosphere, the independently targeted warheads and decoys had the appearance of over 50 incoming weapons. It made them unstoppable.

The sub's communications officer knocked on the captain's door, passing him a priority message.

"Just arrived, Sir. Priority One."

The captain quickly put on his jacket, setting his cap on his head. Then he walked rapidly to the main control center.

"Sound action stations!"

Within a minute, he and his executive officer were seated at their launch desks. They followed the much-practiced drills. Neither showed the emotion they felt; concealing their inner turmoil. Recruits to U.S. "Boomers" were the elite of the Navy. They were highly trained, psychologically screened, and brainwashed. They would do their job, knowing that their homes and families were about to be wiped out.

They blocked out any latent remorse that their own actions would destroy millions of civilians in multiple cities.

The two officers confirmed the launch codes. They turned their two keys. Both thought or hoped it must be a drill or a test of their loyalty. No one would be crazy enough to start WWIII. And why was there to be only one Trident deployed?

The captain knew his duty. He was relieved that the destinations of the warheads would be in code. He would never know whether it was heading for Chinese, Russian, Iranian or other cities. Wherever, those countries had dared to defy the might of the USA. In any case, he knew that the U.S. was the democratic leader of the free world. The President would never give an order to unleash its nukes without good reason.

The executive officer was troubled with visions of his wife and new baby daughter. He would never see them again. He envisioned them evaporated in a holocaust that his action would undoubtedly unleash in retaliation. Maybe they were already dead.

Steeling himself, the captain hit the launch button. He hoped that the Pentagon could still abort after launch. The Trident streaked through the water to the surface in a whoosh of bubbles. Its rockets ignited. The targets were unknown to the crew of the sub. Military shrinks discovered that knowing the targets increased stress and the possibility of refusal to launch.

<<>>

The President of the People's Republic of China sat in his own tense war room. Following his discussion with the President of the United States his forces were on maximum alert. Ground forces were massing on the boarders with Korea. Missiles were aimed at the U.S. seventh fleet, the Philippines, Japan, Singapore and the continental U.S. His Russian allies would deal with NATO.

Critical electronic components in most U.S. military systems originated from China. Frantic efforts to replace them or copy them had largely been subverted. His military advisors wanted him to trigger the secret codes that would make the U.S. blind; its missiles fail and open it to a well-rehearsed Chinese nuclear strike, in conjunction with the Russians.

The Russian President was speaking with him through a translation application on their hotline.

"Our radar shows a cluster of 50 warheads or decoys from a single sea-launched missile. They are all heading to an unpopulated area of the U.S. The U.S. President assured me that this is to take out a rogue operation threatening world peace. All our forces are on high alert. We should wait and see what happens after the warheads land."

The Chinese President told the Russian of the advice of his military.

"They say we should trigger our embedded electronics and strike now. We will never have a better chance."

The Russian responded.

"Let me tell you, Mr. President, our intelligence sources claim that disabling your embedded electronics will still leave maybe 30 percent of U.S. capabilities operational. That will still be enough to destroy us all. We should wait."

For a moment, the Chinese closed his eyes in thought.

"I agree, but at the first sign of attacks on our territory, we launch."

<<>>

The U.S. President was under extreme pressure from her Joint Chiefs of Staff.

"We have 50 incoming warheads, they could still shift targets. Even if not, Phoenix is threatened. We have to launch against China and Russia, before it's too late."

She gave him a stern look.

"No, general, we have to hold our nerve. The presidents of Russia and China have given me their assurances that they will not attack."

"But Madam President, all their forces are on maximum alert."

"So are ours. What the hell would you expect. We hold back!"

The President and her joint chiefs watched their big screen. The cluster of warheads and decoys dispersed above the atmosphere. Then several converged toward their target.

<<>>

In the Minuteman silo, Angelou's face was a numbed but defiant pulp. She was blinded by blood. Her ears were ringing from the blows. Carver was about to take another swing at her. The multiple nuclear warheads pounded one after another onto the roof of the silo. They hammered through the massive ferro-concrete roof like an unimaginably powerful jack hammer.

There were no survivors. The nearby township of Sahuarita was obliterated. Most of the population of Phoenix, Arizona would die from radiation poisoning within weeks.

<<>>

In Sunshine's penitentiary, an hour after the missile exploded, her friendly trustee was back on shift. She delivered a large bag of H.

Sunshine was nearly passing out with shivering desperation.

Minutes later, there was clearly something wrong. Alarms were sounding. Staff were running up and down the corridors, shouting at each other. Sunshine was too far gone in despair to care. She filled the syringe with all the heroin she had; enough for four days. She tightened a cord around her arm. The veins stood out. Finding a gap between previous needle marks, she pushed the needle in. There was the rush, the white light, the euphoria. Then came a sharp stab of pain in her brain. The darkness of terminal oblivion followed.

<<>>

Daremo had heard about the president's address to the terrified U.S. nation following the nuclear explosion in the desert. It was passed off as an accident. Social media reported otherwise till all went off the air.

Japanese people knew what nuclear weapons could do. The entire nation was in panic mode. There were suicides throughout Japan. Mothers killed their children to save them from the holocaust. Daremo seemed unaffected. S/he calmly explained to Bruce what had been broadcast on the radio.

“Bruce-san, we need to be in a remote place, where we can rebuild our work. We will go to Borneo. I will start preparations in the morning.”

<<>>

They spent the night in a small village. The family members already lay dead on the floor when Daremo entered their modest home. They did not want to live through another Hiroshima. Daremo and Bruce shared a modest meal before falling asleep.

<<>>

Bruce considered suicide many times since meeting Daremo. Finally, he decided to execute his plan. Sneaking from a bedroom, he slipped the stolen car into neutral and let it run silently down the hill, so Daremo would not hear him start the engine. The day before he had seen a steel towing cable in the trunk. He tied one end around the bole of a stout oak. He passed the other end through the open driver's window. Then, threading it through the opposite window, he tied it off around another oak.

Trembling slightly, he settled into the driver's seat. He ensured that the metal towline was settled just in front of his neck. He took a deep breath to calm himself. Then he started the engine, gritted his teeth, closed his eyes, and floored the accelerator.

<<>>

Daremo jerked from slumber on hearing the roar followed by tearing metal. S/he rushed outside. S/he found the car a hundred meters up the road. Its engine was still running, after crashing into a tree.

S/he leaned through the window to switch off the engine. There was blood everywhere. Bruce's decapitated head lay on the back seat. It seemed to be looking up at Daremo with bulging eyes. S/he clinically analyzed the situation. *Mmm. When he accelerated, the tow rope tightened. It ripped his head off. Instant death.*

Daremo shrugged. *So, I journey on alone.*

CHAPTER 21

Harmony

Over the 26,000 years after the extinction of mankind, the earth continued its ever-changing state. Continental drift fused new land-masses, tearing others apart. New mountain ranges were thrust skyward by the collisions of tectonic plates and massive volcanic eruptions. The once mighty peaks of the Himalayas and the Rockies were ground down by ice ages, glaciers, and the melting waters. Deserts shifted, disappeared, and reappeared elsewhere. The cities that humans built were gone forever, below the seas, entombed in the earth or swallowed by tropical jungles.

There were craters from asteroids. One had destroyed many species three-thousand years before.

<<>>

Around the world, a powerful collective consciousness held sway. It was formless. It did not reside in any one place. All living things were a part of it. The creatures in the sea, the birds, the insects, the mammals and the reptiles, all had their parts to play. They lived and died as part of the one gigantic organism that cooperated as life on earth.

The planet was especially rich in plant life. Every species had evolved to fill its niche and reclaim the destruction left by people. The plants were the origin and provided the central eco-systems of this collective consciousness. They regulated the atmosphere by varying their co2 emissions. They enabled this by encouraging appropriate species to grow or recede, according to the overall needs of life on earth. They ensured that other species had sufficient food and shelter according to the needs of the era.

The collective memory strengthened. It shared mystical feelings from the distant past. The origin of the current harmony was due to the actions of an inspired hominid. The collective consciousness did not use language, so the nature of this founding spirit was sensed rather than named. Changing the nature of some plants made all that followed possible. It provided the foundations for the current harmony.

<<>>

The collective memory alerted all beings to the lessons of the past. The evil humans of that long-lost era had been eliminated. These wicked ones had tried to destroy the planet. They were from the same hominid species as the founding spirit, but malevolent, rather than benign.

The collective consciousness recalled the damage that humans caused and how they had wreaked destruction across the globe. Strange concepts like tourism, packaging, mining, slash and burn, chemicals, pesticides, herbicides and war were remembered, so as to be avoided in the future. When all life felt itself part of one interconnected entity, there was no need to travel or for any of the other destructive human behaviors.

There was no collective memory of the CRISPR-Cas9 gene splicing technology that Daremo had used. The plants' further evolution was controlled by the collective consciousness and without the need for machines. Because CRISPR-Cas9 had an inherent weakness unknown to Daremo, the intent to destroy all hominids failed. Species with positive characteristics, labeled bonobos, gorillas, gibbons and orangutans by humans were retained. They evolved further. Their enhanced agility, brain capacity and dexterity played important roles in implementing the needs of the collective consciousness. They developed a common language. They used this in the benign service of all beings.

Even after all this time, some plant roots probed into dangerous areas. They discovered nuclear waste stores deep within the earth. Humans had thought it safe. Other plant roots found waste dumps. There, harmful plastics, poisons and gases were still present. Some of these lay beneath the sea bed.

These recollections of hostile, planet-damaging species and their destruction led to remedial actions. Any animals or plants dangerous to the planetary whole had their evolution curtailed or changed. This was managed by regulating food supplies, breeding and through symbiotic rewards and discouragements. Humans and chimps had been identified as harmful and liquidated.

No life-form was dominant. Every form of life was part of the collective whole.
The death of any being was just part of everything. Death created nutrients and recycled resources. These continued as part of other living things.

<<>>

Yet a further 15,000 years on, the collective consciousness developed greater power. Instantaneously, it could project its force and ideas across the universe. It connected with beings on other planets, thousands of light years away in time and space. New knowledge was exchanged. The collective consciousness merged with others to become one with the entire universe.

THE END

Questions for Readers

You may benefit more from discussing this book, if you consider the following questions.

1. If you were born without gender and suffered as Daremo did, how would you feel? To what extent may Daremo's behavior be justified?
2. Given that major elements of human anatomy have only been identified and evaluated in the last 20 years, can we simply write off the scientific evidence around plant sentience as speculation or fantasy?
3. Have there been recent, real life examples of Fake News that have led to catastrophic events, such as Bruce's website does in this novel? Orson Welles' broadcast of a fake news

program about alien invaders in 1938 led to widespread panic and suicides across the U.S. Are we more or less susceptible to such things today and why?

4. Is the description of the Sedona hippy cult compelling? The author knows intelligent people who have been indoctrinated into such delusional societies. Do you?
5. The reactions of the U.S. and other militaries to the events in this novel are frightening. From observing what is occurring around the world today are they realistic?
6. Given the way the current state of the planet and the bleak outlook as a result of human environmental destruction, does the last chapter of this book present a better future for life?

ABOUT THE AUTHOR

Aaron Aalborg is a nom de plume. Born into modest beginnings in the North of England, he has degrees in economics and management and was a visiting Professor at a European Business School for some years. He has wide ranging interests, from world religions to global history, politics, science and martial arts. He worked as an advisor to governments and large businesses all over the world prior to becoming an author. He and his Scottish wife have both worked and lived in Asia, Europe, the U.S. and Latin America.

Published Fiction – Seven previous books by this author have been published by Penman House Publishing. Do visit the website at

http://www.penmanhouse.com/

There is much free material there, including the author's blog. All books are available in e-book and paperback. All are distributed through Amazon. One novel, *Blood-Axe: The Saga of a twenty-First Century Viking*, was published under the name, Chris J Clarke.

WRITTEN AS AARON AALBORG

They Deserved It - Both a historical and contemporary novel, it is based on a true story about women poisoning their husbands in 17th Century Italy. It is a fast-moving thriller. There is a cast of abused young women, rascally husbands, witches, evil cardinals, and a horrible Pope. The discovery of a mysterious Egyptian box moves the story into contemporary New York. There, a rogue lawyer and her lesbian lover, the head of an IT company, continue the murders. There is a thrilling pursuit around the world, before the unexpected finale.

Revolution - A thrilling account of the assassination of multiple heads of state, including the U.S. President and the British royal family. It is set in the near future. A socialist revolution and world-wide mayhem follow. The U.S. and the world descend into chaos. There is furious action and a dramatic terminal twist.

Doom, Gloom and Despair - A collection of short stories including dramas around failed rebellions, packs of ravenous dogs, volcanic eruptions, dueling deities and a suicide cult. These sardonically dark stories feature man-eating animals, cannibals and other bleak events. Perfect for potential suicides and those of sensitive disposition, or perhaps not.

Cooking the Rich, A Post-Revolutionary Necessity - This spoof cookbook includes hilarious recipes for cooking Donald Trump, The British Royal Family, billionaires and Middle Eastern potentates. The author still wonders why he is still alive.

Terminated - The Making of a Serial Killer - volume one - from the slums to the Falklands War - In this thriller Alex, a poor boy from Scotland and a martial artist, beats the odds to win a top education. He becomes a successful businessman. Recruited by a crack special services unit, he is embroiled in the Falklands War with Argentina. He returns an unsung hero. There is non-stop excitement. His personal life is equally dramatic.

Terminated - The Making of a Serial Killer - volume two - from hero to serial killer - Alex returns to a stellar international business career. He soon becomes embroiled in the evils of the business world. He meets psychopaths in politics, through top management consulting, and in investment banking. After murders and assassinations, he becomes CEO of an executive search firm. He discovers that headhunting is as corrupt as everything else. After trying to fight his demons in a Buddhist monastery, he returns like an avenging angel to eliminate those he feels deserve it.

WRITTEN AS CHRIS J CLARKE

Blood-Axe: The Saga of a 21st Century Viking - Many readers are fascinated by tales about the Vikings. They allow us to escape into an exciting bygone era, unencumbered by the inconvenient restrictions of tedious civilization.

Blood-Axe is a modern fantasy tale of men and women who form a Viking re-enactment group. Carried away, they destroy an English town amidst witchcraft, blood sacrifice, slaughter, rape and pillage.

It is a rollicking mix of hilariously crazy scenes; scary social comment on the inner Viking within all of us and a cliff hanging thriller with a most unusual plot.

Coming in 2019

Tales of a Misspent Life - This is the working title for a series of entertaining, scandalous, and hilarious true stories and anecdotes from around the world.

Ryan By K. Francis Ryan

A Penman House Author

The Echoes Quartet

Echoes Through the Mist –

Book I in the Echoes Quartet

Julian Blessing is rescued from a life on Wall Street that is killing him. He possesses extraordinary paranormal abilities—abilities he doesn't realize he has until he is confronted by madness and evil on the rocky coast of Ireland.

Echoes Through the Vatican –

Book II in the Echoes Quartet

Greed, corruption, money laundering and murder—that's what awaits Julian Blessing in The Eternal City. Rome is Julian's destination, but often the reasons we go somewhere are not the reasons we need to be there. Then there is the Jesuit Book. It is a book that shouldn't exist, that many hope doesn't exist and that people will kill to possess.

Echoes from the Past –

Book III in the Echoes Quartet

Julian Blessing is back on Ireland's fog-cloaked coast. He has to build up hisparanormal defenses if he hopes to protect an age-old treasure. Faltering in his mission will bring chaos to the world and everything Julian holds dearer than his life will be lost.

Echoes Through Time –

Book IV in the Echoes Quartet

Julian Blessing has returned to the peaceful village of Cappel Vale. Below the surface however a secret is harbored—a secret that involves a heinous crime from the distant past and its present-day punishment. The criminal has been found, sentence has been passed, but protecting the identity of the executioner is essential to the welfare of the village.

An evil from Julian's past has returned for revenge. Failure to expunge the malevolence will cost Julian everything and everyone he loves.

23992592R00170

Printed in Great Britain
by Amazon